First published in Great Britain in 2011 by Comma Press
www.commapress.co.uk

First published in Stockholm as *Brorsan är matt* by Norstedts, 2007.

The moral rights of Mirja Unge to be identified as the Author of this Work, and of Kari Dickson to be identified as the Translator of this Work, have been asserted in accordance with the Copyright Designs and Patents Act 1988.

A CIP catalogue record of this book is available from the British Library.

ISBN   1905583370
ISBN-13   978 1905583379

LOTTERY FUNDED

The publisher gratefully acknowledges assistance from the Arts Council England North West. With the support of the Culture Programme (2007-2013) of the European Union.

Education and Culture DG

Culture

Culture Programme

This project has been funded with support from the European Commission. This publication reflects the views only of the author, and the Commission cannot be held responsible for any use which may be made of the information contained therein.

Set in Bembo 11/13 by David Eckersall
Printed and bound in England by Short Run Press.

IT WAS JUST, YESTERDAY

by
Mirja Unge

Translated by
Kari Dickson

Contents

It Was Just, Yesterday

IF I RUN for it at five to eight I just make the bus, and that mongol kid is sitting there as usual, playing King of the Bus. He goes all the way to the special school at the last stop and sits there shouting the whole way. He does it every morning when you get on, and does it this morning too, of course.

Welcome onboard the bus, you with the black hair, he shouts, because he keeps an eye on everyone on the bus, his tongue hanging out a bit.

Where d'you get the air from, I say, when I get to the back of the bus where he's sitting, with his legs apart and hair combed flat, and I don't even need to look in his direction because, let's face it, I've seen him before. He laughs and slaps his bus pass on his thigh, and I sit down a few seats in front of him and check my hair in a small mirror, jet black around my face. There's one stop between me and Thea and when I dyed it she'd said, man, your hair's really cool. It suited me black, Thea said, and she pulled her fingers through it.

The bus pulls in by the church and Thea and her brother get on, and Thea has cropped all her hair so that her neck and throat, you can't keep your eyes off them. Welcome onboard, shouts the King of the Bus, and Thea has painted her lips purple. Thanks, she says, and sits down on the seat opposite me. Where d'you get the air from, says the King of the Bus. I just took it, didn't I, simple, Thea says.

Thea and I roll cigarettes on the bus, and the tobacco crumbles and slips between our fingers, and Thea has earrings

1

with skulls, lined up right the way round her earlobe, and I laugh. Why are you laughing, Thea says. Aw, it was just, yesterday, I say. Did you get any, then, she says, and sits with her back to the window and stretches her legs out over the seat with her trainers sticking out into the aisle. No feet on the seat, roars the King of the Bus, and Thea snorts and so do I. Didn't do very well, though, I say. Did you not get any, then, Thea says, and I shrug because for two bloody hours I'd stood outside the off-licence and tried to get someone to buy something for me. The best ones are usually the young guys who you can hang around and giggle with, so that they warm to you, and start to ask for your phone number, and I normally give them the maths teacher's number because I've learnt it off by heart now. It was just that when I was standing there, trying, this alky came along and asked what I wanted, and I gave him two hundred, and my feet were so cold they were freezing. And then some guys came and started talking to me, and I kept an eye on the door to the off-licence, I did, but he never came out, and I didn't get it because he'd gone in, hadn't he, but he didn't come out, and then they shut, and one of the guys, he'd bought a whole lot of wine and said I could get a bottle from him, and that was pretty cool, really. Just some bum who buggered off with my money, I say to Thea on the bus. Never, really, she says. But I got some wine from another guy, so that was cool, I say to Thea, and she says fuck, he legged it with two hundred kronor.

The bus brakes suddenly for an elk or something, some deer that's bolted over the road and into the forest, and Thea rolls cigarettes. Thea has painted her nails green and she's got this scent about her that's in everything that's hers, her clothes, her room and her hair, lovely and soft, it's there. Fucking hell, he made off with two hundred, Thea says. Yeah, but at least I got some wine, I say. Was it red wine then, Thea says. I don't know. Didn't you check, she says, and I look out of the window and say that I left it at his place. What? I left it at his place, I say, and she fixes her eyes on me, and they're green with brown speckles in the middle and she's got black mascara on and she's got this allergy and is always bunged up.

The bus slows down by the market garden and all the people waiting push and jostle each other to get on. Welcome onboard, shouts the King of the Bus, and I scream shut up. Where d'you get the air from, he says. She just gets it, don't you see, says Thea, and the bus pulls out and moves back onto the road.

Thea's eyes pierce me. You went to his place, she says, and I nod and she gathers up the tobacco and her bag and everything and comes over and sits down beside me, and I move up and into the sphere of scent that surrounds her. I can feel that my feet are totally cold and stiff, the bones as heavy as they were when I went home with him, because he said I should go up to his for a while, he was absolutely certain that he knew who the wino was who'd run off with my money, so if I went up with him he'd phone round and check it out, because I did want the money back, didn't I, and he was totally convinced that he knew who the guy who nicked the money was. He rattled on about the alky who was obviously off his head and I walked beside him and I didn't need to, I could get the bus home and phone Thea, have her voice in my ear, almost inside me, but I walked beside him and was cold and listened to his chat and the bottles clinking against each other in the box he was carrying. He punched in the door code and pushed open the front door and I went in after him, up the stairs, and I could have turned but I didn't turn, and I waited behind him while he unlocked his door.

Really, Thea says, and nudges me and I wiggle my toes because there's no life in my feet. Yeah, can you believe it, I grin, this fucking awful bedsit with an eighties-style fan on the ceiling, like, and a fitted carpet, I say. And it was freezing outside and warm in his flat and he poured some whisky and I drank it, and it warmed me up inside and all over, and I giggled and felt warm, but my feet were cold, my feet were freezing. He'd phone the bum later, he said, but first he'd put on some music. Iron Maiden, he put on, and the whisky made everything spin as I hadn't eaten anything since lunch at school, and I didn't think, I didn't realise, until he was sitting on the sofa with me and he had on some aftershave, and he worked with computers for a company somewhere, and he stroked his hand over my hair, and it felt so good with his hand on my hair.

What did you do at his, then, Thea says, and licks the glue on the cigarette paper. Drank whisky, I say. It's amazing how quickly whisky goes to your head, I laugh, and Thea laughs too, and her tits bounce under her top because she doesn't believe in restricting things in bras and cages, and she's a vegetarian and sometimes screams at the old ladies in town in furs. And the evening before last, when we were sitting up in Thea's room in the attic, with the sloping ceiling so you can't sit upright on the bed, we were lying there, laughing, and I said your tits bounce up and down when you laugh.

You'd better not be lying there looking at my tits, she said. Why not, they're just there, aren't they, bobbing and bouncing? How can I avoid looking at them, I said. Well, Thea said, they're not that big. Nah, that's true, I said. Are they small, then, she said, and pushed up on her elbow. Nah, not really, I said. But you think they're small, don't you, she said, and pulled up her top so that her breasts were taken totally by surprise and lay there in their whiteness. So you think they're small, she said, and squeezed and weighed one with her hand. I leant over and put my hand, carefully placed my hand, so the palm touched and pressed down on her and the breast that was almost hot. So they're too small, aren't they, Thea said, and I pulled back my hand and found some saliva to wet my throat. They're just the way they should be, I said, in fact I'm sure that that's exactly how they should be, really. She pulled down her top and sat on the edge of the bed. They might still grow a bit more, she said. And I sit there on the bus and watch her laugh, and I look at her eyes.

The bus drives past the pig farm and the stench of pigs seeps in through the windows and the cracks, filling every breath, and the King of the Bus smirks at the back and shouts out who's farting on the bus?

Shut your mouth, I scream, and Thea takes her little perfume bottle out of her bag and sprays it around in the air.

Was he good-looking, then, the guy, Thea says, and I try to remember what I can about his looks, because everyone looks like something, and you just need to remember but I couldn't remember, I could only remember him smiling when we were standing out in the kitchen and I asked if he was going to ring that alky who'd nicked my money, how he smiled then, and said that I was so sweet, and Thea says that sometimes too, sometimes she comes and gives me a hug and sometimes she laughs and wants a kiss, and when I was there in his kitchen he suddenly leant over and kissed me on the mouth and I didn't have time to see it coming or realise before he was kissing me, and then it was over and I tottered a bit and he held me because he had very strong arms and a white T-shirt with the Lacoste crocodile on.

Go on then, what did he look like, Thea says on the bus, and I shrug. Maybe he was good looking. I don't understand how you could forget the bottle of wine, she says. What, I say. The bottle of wine, how could you leave the bottle of wine at his place? Oh, I must've been too drunk, I say and laugh, and she laughs too and the bus rattles along and I forgot the bottle of wine. I wasn't thinking about it, just walked away, walked slowly because it was hurting somewhere, it was empty, and this massive fucking loneliness just started to grow and grow and I couldn't understand, I didn't know, because I hadn't said anything, I hadn't tried to get away from his body, I just lay there on the sofa and

5

something exploded in my belly and my cunt when he pushed in, and Iron Maiden screamed and my head thumped against the arm of the sofa, thump thump against the arm, and I said nothing, I did nothing, but I was there, with my head pressed against the arm of the sofa and Iron Maiden and the whisky in my head, thump thump. My feet walked, as they could and should, across the asphalt to the bus stop, but I forgot the bottle of wine, I'd forgotten it, and I knew that I'd forgotten something, it was just I couldn't remember what.

He took my virginity, I said. Well, then you beat me to it, Thea hisses. I press the stop button and the bus pulls into the turning place by the school. Welcome aboard again tomorrow, shouts the King of the Bus, and I turn round and scream where d'you get the air from?

Well what was it like then, Thea says, and tugs at my arm, and I shrug and look out through the window.

Alright I suppose.

Oranges

It was nice of them to come and, like, bother about the fact you're turning eighteen and that. I hadn't really thought about it, just stood there in the door and they sang happy birthday and Anita got all soppy and was running around now, in her dressing gown, putting on the coffee and making breakfast. And they'd got Linus with them too, stood there in the hallway in his snow-covered trainers with ten bloody roses that he'd bought, and he held them out and he hugged me and I hadn't showered or washed my hair so it just hung lank and looked greasy, I thought, but it didn't seem to bother him because he nuzzled in, even though I kind of froze a bit. And Sara took Vicke out of the cage where he was dozing, because she liked having him on her lap and he liked it too and sat there grinding his teeth when she scratched him between the ears and he was bloody overweight even though Anita had had him on a diet for ages now.

Mum hadn't met Linus, though I'd told her I hung out with him, so she knew about him and all that, and now he was sitting there, on the bench in the kitchen where we usually sat, Anita and me, now he was sitting there, and he smuggled the snus[1] out of his mouth and back into the tin. And Sara and Magda had presents and things that they piled up on the table and Anita had got some clothes on and was sitting, smoking under the fan, and offered her yellow Blend cigarettes to everyone but no one wanted one. Magda rolled her John Silver and sat down with Anita by the fan and Linus drank his coffee and looked at me and gave me a knowing

1. A form of chewing tobacco common throughout Sweden.

smile and Sara sat there, feeding Vicke crispbread, so he was happy as a pig in shit because no one bothered about him otherwise. Linus stretched his hand out under the table and stroked my knee and Anita said she thought it was really nice to meet Linus as well because I've heard so much about you, she said, and Linus gave a lopsided smile and stroked my knee. Aren't you going to open them then, Magda said, and I played with my fringe and it was really nice of them to get presents and all that, so I picked the smallest one and unwrapped some really cool earrings with the peace sign on, and then I realised what was in the other one when I gave it a shake, and Magda grinned and Linus packed some snus and put it in and wiped his fingers on his jeans. I started to unwrap the second present and Anita shuffled around barefoot in her Scholls and put some buns in the oven to defrost. I pulled the paper off and there was a tape inside, and how Magda'd got me a tape of Eddie Medusa I don't know, but it was a brand new tape and she grinned and said that it was a fucking good recording, much better than the one I've got, she said, and Anita wondered what it was and said that I should put it on the cassette player, there in the kitchen, but no fucking way, I thought. Anita put the buns down on the table and Linus and Sara started to eat. Jesus, thanks, I said, and nice of you to come and all that, and I held Linus' hand under the table, kind of warm and sweaty it was, and he sneaked a smile and slurped his coffee and flicked his blond fringe, his eyes brown below. Really nice of you to come, I said, because I realised that they must've got up early to take the bus out here and sacrificed a lie-in and all that. And Magda grinned and blew smoke up into the fan because it had probably been her idea to come here and to drag Linus along too, and he hadn't been here yet, even though we'd been together since the beginning of December. Magda had some wool with her and was going to plait me a friendship bracelet because she made really fucking cool ones. She got out her wool and I had to choose the colours and it was going to be a totally cool black and white one. Magda tied the wool to a safety pin and fixed it to her jeans and started to twist the wool and she was so fucking good at getting the pattern and all that. And Linus was comfortable on the kitchen bench and looked like he sat there all the time, drinking Anita's coffee. They all seemed to be getting on fine so I nipped out to the toilet and sprayed my hair and put on some mascara and when I came back again Anita was sitting, leaning forwards so she could see down the road, and I leant forwards as well and saw someone cycling down the road and it was wonky, I mean the bike was wonky as hell, and it was still icy right out to the main road. Look, there's someone coming down here on a bicycle, Anita said, and stubbed out her cigarette and leant forwards. Wow, your dad's coming too now, Anita said, and pulled another fag out of the packet. Could be anyone, that, I said. I mean, we had neighbours, didn't we. We didn't live in total fucking isolation. It is him, Anita said, so Lennart's got the bike out, obviously, and has come all the way over here, she said, and I saw that it was him cycling towards us, slowly slipping down the icy road, and the new kid was on the back, the new kid was sitting on the back, glaring out from under a sheepskin hat. And he's got the new kid with him, Anita said. No doubt he wants to say happy birthday to you. That's probably why he's cycled over here, because he's never had a driving licence and he obviously can't afford to take the bus, Anita said, and I knew only too well and so did everyone else in the town, for that matter, that Lennart cycles, and he's almost always hanging around in town with his bike. Ah, there's Linda's dad coming now, Anita said, and I said to her to sit by the fan and smoke and not wander around all over the place, because it stinks of cigarettes in here now, I said. And Magda and Sara looked out of the window at Lennart and saw him slipping on the ice. Is that your dad, Magda said, and leant forward and stared. I didn't know that he was your dad, she said, and I mean she'd obviously seen him before, though they hadn't actually met, but they'd seen him around town with his bike. Standing there all the time, he was, with his bike, outside the supermarket, staring and saying hello to the people who went in. Linus spread another piece of bread and sat there and chewed and was always bloody hungry, he was, and Vicke sat grinding his teeth on Sara's lap, and I saw Lennart brake and slide on his bike on the icy road outside, and then he lifted the new kid off and locked up the bike and he had this bloody great basket on the handlebars. You won't have met Linda's dad, Anita said, and I said that she should cut more bread because Linus wanted more, didn't he, I said, and Linus grinned and said if there was any, well. The doorbell rang and there was a knock on the door and I skidded out into the hall in my woolly socks and opened the door and Lennart was standing there, smiley and bright, and the new kid was behind him all snotty in her waterproofs. Well, Lennart said, and nodded down at the new kid, now we can say happy birthday to Linda, he said, talking down to the new kid. Really nice of you to come, I said, and he barged into the hall with his basket and I peeked in and he'd obviously gone to town, Lennart, and packed it full of presents. Yes, he was smiling away, and the new kid was holding on to his trouser leg. Come on in then, I said, and he wiped away the new kid's snot with his hand. Should we go in, he asked the new kid, bending down, and I said of course they should come in. Is he coming in, Anita called from the kitchen, and Lennart bent down slowly and pulled the new kid's boots off. Well, they've asked us in now, Lennart said to the kid, and he didn't have a jacket on, I noticed, just several sweaters that he started to peel off. The layered method, I said, and he bent down over the kid and said well, we'd better go in now, and he obviously didn't have any money, Dad didn't have money, but he had layers of sweaters instead and he was standing there peeling them off, and underneath it all he was really sinewy and skinny as he walked across the floor with the kid hanging onto his trouser leg. Well, let's go into the kitchen then, he said to the kid, and I followed behind. Lennart lifted the new kid up onto the sofa, so there sat the kid, staring at Vicke who was perched crunching crispbread on Sara's lap. Lennart had holes under the arms of his innermost t-shirt, I noticed, and Linus sat and chewed on his sandwich and Magda sat by the fan smoking and plaiting the wool bracelet and Lennart looked at them for a while but he didn't say anything, even though they said hello to him, and Lennart stared back and Linus started to fidget with his snus and Madga lit another. There's other people here, Lennart said to the new kid. It's Linda's friends who're sitting here, you see, he said, and the kid sat there and squirmed in her waterproofs and was too bloody hot, I reckon. Oh, we've forgotten the basket, Lennart said, and went out to get it. Anita sat on the worktop with a cigarette and I said that she should hold it under the fan because it stinks of fags in here now, I said, and Lennart came in with the basket and cleared a space on the table for it, and Linda's eighteen now, you see, Lennart said to the new kid. You've got a lot with you there, Linus said, and Lennart smiled and stretched over and buttered a piece of bread, and he found some old mugs on the draining board and emptied one and filled it with coffee and stood there drinking. And it was quiet, just the whir of the fan and Vicke grinding his teeth when Sara pulled his ears and scratched them, and the basket stood there, big and full on the table, and he'd cycled out here with it. Really nice of you to come, I said, and he smiled and sort of raised his eyebrows and he got sick pay, only he didn't have any money, to come here with such a big basket, I said, and he smiled. But we'd like the basket back later, wouldn't we, he said to the new kid, and well of course he'd get it back, I understood that, I said, and I mean what would I do with it anyway? The new kid squirmed in her waterproofs and Linus searched for my hand under the table, a sweaty and warm hand he had, and he held mine. Anita said why don't we put on that tape, even though there was no fucking way we were going to. Oh well, said Anita, and sat there on the worktop tipping her shoe. And Magda eyed up the basket and said well, go on then, are you not going to open them, she said, and of course I would, wouldn't I. Couldn't it wait a while, or was there a rush, I said, and I didn't know how much time they had or how long they could stay and, I mean, hang out. Sara leant over towards the new kid and undid the zip on her rain jacket and the new kid started to take it off and Lennart smiled and said so you're getting help to take off your waterproofs. And should we help Linda to open her presents, he said to the kid, and stretched over and took one out of the basket and the kid pulled at the string and paper and suddenly an orange rolled out onto the table and Linus and Magda started to laugh their heads off and the kid stared at them and Anita sat on the worktop and tapped the ash from her cigarette and tipped her shoe on her toe. Give Linda a present, Lennart said to the kid, and the kid reached over and got hold of a present and gave it to me and that's nice, I said to the kid, and pulled at the string around the present and unwrapped another orange, and Madga and Linus laughed like before. Bloody good idea that, the oranges, Magda said, and Sara giggled and Anita lit up another cigarette and ran her thumb over her lower lip. And the kid handed me another present and I could feel that it was, well, round, I don't know, and I unwrapped an orange and Magda giggled and Sara asked if she could get one and of course she could. I went and got the coffee pot and asked if anyone wanted any, and Lennart held out his mug and I said to him that he could take a clean mug, because Anita had been drinking buttermilk from that one, I said, but Lennart smiled and winked and Magda said aren't you going to unwrap them all, then, and of course I am, but there isn't any rush, is there, and no need to bloody stress, I said, and Magda shrugged and rolled another John Silver and Anita took a drag and blew the smoke at the window and I said that she might as well open the window now, if she was going to blow smoke in that direction, otherwise it won't get out, I said. Okay, okay, Anita said, and opened the window and I sat down at the table again and took out another present and pulled at the string and unwrapped an orange that rolled out and over to the others, and Sara was sitting there giggling and peeling now, and Linus grinned and Magda thought it was a really cool idea, she said, and lit up her John Silver and I unwrapped another one that rolled away and the paper fell onto the floor and the string, and the new kid just stared and Lennart nodded and smiled and said to the kid that Linda's eighteen now, you see, Lennart said, and I unwrapped the presents and the oranges rolled all over the table and then lay still and Linus stopped grinning and packed in some snus and Anita sat balancing her Scholl shoe on her toe and I unwrapped oranges, one after the other, I unwrapped them and they rolled out of the paper and lay there shiny and orange on the table. Sara asked if she could peel one for the kid as well, and of course she can have one, and you too, I said, you can have one too. And there were only a few parcels left at the bottom now, and I picked them out and unwrapped them. Linus sat with his lip stretched over the snus and Sara chewed her orange while she peeled another and Mum dropped her slipper and fished it up again with her toe. I took the last present out of the basket and unwrapped it and is that the last one, Sara said, and I nodded and Linus sat with his mouth open and stared as I unwrapped it. I pulled off the string and unwrapped the last orange and it rolled out onto the table and lay there with the rest. There was silence and Magda got up and looked in the basket and then sat down again. The fan whirred and I reached for the last orange and started to peel it. Really nice of you to come, I said, and Lennart smiled. Magda sat and plaited the wool bracelet and kept her eyes on it and Linus had obviously taken a large pinch of snus and was numbed by it.

The Attic

FRIDA SAT OPPOSITE me in the café and licked the corners of her mouth when she'd finished her pastry. She liked pastries, I could tell. I sat and stirred my coffee and lit up a cigarette and didn't really know why I'd applied to college and was about to start studying. I'd met Frida at registration and after the first lecture we'd gone to find the reading list in the library and she wanted to show me around the town because I didn't really know the town and she did and wanted to show it to me and of course she had a fine old time.

Frida licked the spoon and pushed her glasses up on her nose, and I'd seen her eyes when she took her glasses off, big and brown they were, but now they were small and shrunken behind the glasses, and I said that I was looking for somewhere to rent because I couldn't keep commuting from my dad's and it would be pure bliss not to have to deal with him anymore as well, I said, and she nodded. We could share somewhere if you like, I said, because I mean it would be cheaper, and maybe it was a bit cheeky as I didn't know her and she didn't know me. But she nodded and said that she'd like to, if we could find somewhere.

We wondered around in town and bought some papers and sat and read through the adverts, and a few days later we went to see the attic flat because it sounded really nice and it was cheap. Open and bright it was, with only one big room, but if we divided it up a bit, she said, and I nodded and looked out through the window. You can see right to the church, I said.

Later we sat in a café and made some plans as I didn't

have much furniture, except for a stereo, of course, and some china that I could weed out from the cupboards at home. And she hadn't lived away from home before either, but her dad had rented out flats, so obviously had furniture that he could fix up and take over and that would be as cool as, I said.

The owners ran the paper shop on the ground floor, so we went there and signed the contract and we'd never done anything like that before, but we wrote our names side by side in the square at the top and the owners gave us the keys and the shop door tinkled when we went back out into the late summer and it was really humid. We bought a six-pack and sat in the park and drank beer and ate cherries and the geese came and hissed and begged and we threw cherry stones at them.

It's really nice of you, I said to Frida's dad a few days later, when he turned up at the flat with a trailer load of things and he shook my hand and stood there by the car. He was grey and short and limp-handed, and my dad was tall, I guess, not one of the sort you could stand and look down at and totter around in your high heels. I dropped my cigarette in a puddle and started to take things down from the trailer and carry them up the stairs, because it was an old building with no lift, and it was heavy and awkward with the beds on the winding stairs, and I hadn't lived in a flat before, but now I was going to, and Dad thought it was high time I moved out because he'd moved away from home when he was sixteen or something like that and I didn't really want to stay with him anymore either. I'd been home and dug out some pans and things but I hadn't got much other than the stereo, but Frida's dad had beds and a table and chairs. Really nice of you, I said to Frida's dad, as he carried one end of the bed and I carried the other, and Frida's dad had trousers with a centre crease and the sweat shone on his crown, and my dad didn't have a centre crease or a bald patch, in fact he had loads of really thick hair, my dad, that stuck out everywhere and I cut it for him every now and then. Later Frida's dad wanted a coffee, and sat down on one of the chairs and drank it, and Frida and I went through things and sorted them out. And then her dad got up and was about to leave, and he was so short, and I stood there and looked down at his bald patch and said thank you so much for everything, I said, really nice of you. And he looked up at me and said that he wanted a thousand kronor for the furniture and petrol. I stood there and stared at him and started to kind of shake and Frida just carried on unpacking things and putting them away in a cupboard. You have spoken to your parents, haven't you, he said, but I didn't know what I was supposed to have spoken to my dad about. And of course I'd thought of chipping in with some petrol money, but I hadn't known that he'd want a thousand kronor, and I could have bought a table and chairs at a jumble sale for that price instead. A thousand kronor, I said, I can't afford that. Bringing it up afterwards was kind of sneaky. Then, I don't know, he changed his tune somehow and said that we could just forget about the money and thank you very much for being so helpful and carrying so much, he said, and the corners of his mouth twitched. Frida went down with him and I stood and watched them down by the car, his white crown and her fair ponytail. I looked around the room and there were his beds and I was going to lie in one of them and there were his chairs and I was going to sit on them.

The rain started to patter on the skylight and I was wandering around between the furniture when she came back up and I said that he should have said before because then I could've said no that I didn't want the stuff, shouldn't he, I said to her. She unpacked the china and when you bring it up afterwards well then you don't have any choice, I said, and she shrugged. I mean, he came for your sake as well, you're going to live here too, aren't you, I said. Yes, but you didn't have to pay in the end, she said, and I wandered around amongst the things and unpacked, and I'd brought things from home too so it wasn't just her things and I don't know, but it would have been nice to be able to phone and talk to someone and ask whether I should pay all the same, but I knew what Dad was like and that he wouldn't help anyone except reluctantly. My dad wasn't exactly someone you phoned. I opened the skylight a bit and sat under it and had a cigarette and Frida pottered about unpacking.

I had never lived with anyone like that before, so close. In the evening she went to bed before me and lay quietly in her corner, and I sat under the skylight and smoked. It was the skylight I liked best, sitting there watching the clouds and listening to the rain, and sometimes a thick fog lay everywhere. And every morning she asked me if I'd slept well and I couldn't understand why she always wanted to know and I didn't know how to answer her every morning either, because Dad and I didn't say that sort thing to each other, all forced. And she was an early bird, tidying up the dishes in the sink, so I became an early bird too and woke up when she was getting dressed, and every night I saw her pull off her jeans and take off her top and hang them on the chair, and in the morning I saw her doing up her bra and adjusting her tits and she saw me. In the mornings we stood in the bathroom and put on our makeup and crammed in front of the mirror and borrowed and tried each other's things and showered and scrubbed each other's backs, and I washed the short chubby rolls of her back and she washed my long, muscly one. And when we had lectures we got the bus together to college. And she liked making food and Dad and I had never made much food, I mean Dad sometimes made a stew that lasted for days, but Frida, she made suppers and all sorts of dishes. And she loved desserts and was always whipping them up, and Dad and I never ate things like that, though sometimes he bought pastries on Sundays. And we sat there in the evenings and ate and talked about things and it was so bloody easy to talk to her because she just sat there and listened and asked questions and always had something to say, because she was more experienced than me and I didn't really know much. And I hadn't told anyone about Emil before, but now it just came out, I sat there and it poured out of me, that I'd caught him with this girl later. Shit, I didn't talk about Dad, but then I never usually talked about Dad. And Dad hadn't phoned since I moved there and probably wouldn't phone, either. Phoning's not really Dad's thing, you see, I said to Frida and she nodded.

I popped down to the shop to buy cigarettes all the time, and say hello to one of the landlords' wives, the one who worked there most with green mascara and a perm, and she was nice and gave me sweets and stood and smoked with me out on the step and told me about the house and who lived there.

And we'd got into the habit of going to the college bar so some Friday nights we sat there and drank beer and Ida from our class sat with us. She had been up to our place a few times, Ida, and she thought we'd been friends for ages but we hadn't, and Frida smiled at me and raised her glass and we were so bloody different but that was cool, that we were different, and she had something that was kind of new. We went back to our place when they closed and Frida was tired and went to sleep and Ida and I sat under the skylight and smoked and drank wine.

And it was one of those winters that was always threatening to come but then no proper winter came, just fog that lay heavy and pushed down against the skylight. And every month the invoice for the rent dropped through the letterbox and for the first few months we paid at the bank. But then Frida had said that her dad could fix it so we wouldn't need to pay the bank charges every time. I knew nothing about things like that because I'd never paid rent before, just used to leave some money for Dad in his tin at home whenever

I'd had a job and earned something. But Frida's dad worked in a bank, didn't he, and obviously had opportunities and all that and we were friends again, him and me, and he came by some weekends for a coffee, which was really nice. And it was pretty cool that we wouldn't have to pay the charges, because I didn't want to be paying charges all the time really. So I gave her the rent every month and she gave it to her dad because he was a bank manager and was at the bank and sat there doing things I knew nothing about.

It was Saturday and Frida was off visiting some relatives, and I ran down the stairs and bought some cigs in the shop and talked to Mrs Landlord and chewed on some toffees she'd given me and the snow was coming down and melting straightaway. I wandered around town in the snow, smoking and freezing, and then I saw Ida, it was Ida up ahead of me, so I ran to catch up with her. And Ida was on her way to some party and wondered if I wanted to tag along. Of course I fucking did, I said, and she smiled and we went to buy beer and she had a half bottle in her bag as well. We sat on the bus on the way out to the party and put on some makeup and drank from the half bottle, and she had eyeliner and mascara that I could borrow.

It was some girl with black hair who opened the door, and Ida already knew a whole load of people and we sat there at the party with all these people and drank beer and downed the half bottle. And I don't know, but anyway, it was fucking late and we sat on the night bus back into town and hung around and felt sick. I staggered up the stairs to the attic and slipped the key into the lock. The moon was suspended above the skylight and I turned on the tap for some water, which I drank, and then I heard her voice in the corner. Where have you been? And I started to shake, and I don't know, I was totally pissed and cold, and I said that I'd been to the party with Ida, and she didn't say anything, just the clunking of the fridge, and I was freezing and my teeth were chattering.

THE ATTIC

I was woken by her clattering in the kitchenette and her heels hard on the floor. My head was thumping and she didn't look at me when I sat down opposite her at the table, and she had her glasses on so her eyes were small and shrunken behind them. And I said that it had been totally spontaneous and I'd just bumped into Ida in town, I said, and she said nothing. You weren't at home and we can do different things sometimes, can't we, I said, and she carried on reading and turned the page. I was shaking and felt sick and of course it was stupid of me, I said, I should have phoned or something, but then I didn't want to wake you or anything and I didn't know how late I'd be, I said, and tried to get a few spoonfuls of yoghurt in me and she pushed up her glasses and turned the page and read on. I'm sorry, I am, I said, it's rubbish that it turned out like that, really shitty of me, I said, and she lifted her gaze and said it's your turn to hoover. And of course I could do it, couldn't I, though I didn't think you needed to hoover all the time, but we were quite different like that. Me and my dad didn't hoover very often. At most we swept the kitchen every now and then. I was shaking and pulled the hoover around and the sleet slapped on the skylight.

Ida started coming to the flat all the time and hanging out and playing cards. We sat there and drank wine and chatted and Frida made chocolate mousse which we ate, then licked our spoons. And we had a kitty that we put money in and used for what we bought together, and Ida thought we were like an old couple, she said, and I had never spoken to anyone before like I did to Frida and of course we were different but I liked that about her, that she was different, and that was probably what she liked about me. I liked listening to what was different about her, and I couldn't make food before, I mean Dad hadn't taught me, but Frida, she had recipes and things and helped me, so we stood there and made food together and sometimes when we sat down and ate it, afterwards I thought Dad should taste this, that I could make this for him sometime. And Frida, she knew all about wines and grapes and regions, and we stood there making food and drinking wine from different countries and places.

It was strange that the invoices for the rent stopped coming in the post and I asked her about it when there hadn't been any for ages. But she didn't know anything about it either. How should I know, you ask about everything all the time, she said, and I said I was just wondering and that she didn't need to be like that, but she was obviously menstrual or had indigestion or something.

We sat there in the evenings and talked and I didn't feel uneasy at first but then later it started to sneak in, the uneasiness. God, I'm just sitting here nattering away, I said. Doesn't matter, she said, and of course it didn't exactly matter but she got quieter and I sat there and talked and talked. And I wasn't that exact with the kitty, either. I did the shopping and put the receipt in the tin, but she started to sit there with all the receipts and calculate and go through them. Then when I was going to the offie one time, I noticed that it was nearly empty. But we put money in just recently, I said to her, but then she'd bought something I didn't know about and she was really pissed off with me because she'd told me clearly that she was going to buy something and I'd obviously forgotten. And I didn't want to ask for the receipt or anything and I couldn't face nagging her when she was like that and I didn't really care about the change and Dad always said what goes around comes around and you just have to trust, he said, and that if you've got money you should use it. He never had enough money, Dad, but he bet on the horses and usually when we were scraping the bottom of the barrel he would win on the horses so we'd get pizza and beer and eat the most amazingly expensive pizza with beef and béarnaise sauce.

Later we sat there doing our assessments, ten fucking pages it was, and we'd bought sweets and snacks and sat there and studied, and she had a computer that she let me borrow because I didn't have a computer, though Dad had some ancient electric typewriter that he used sometimes. Really nice of her to let me write the final copy on her computer. I sat and tried to log on, but it didn't seem to be working. I don't know, there must be something wrong, I said to her. Frida was sitting there studying with her glasses on and she kept pushing them up because they seemed to keep slipping. She got up and bent down over the computer and said that she had a new password. Have you got a new password, I asked, because I knew the old one, she'd told me it and I knew it. Yes, she said, and bent over and typed in the new one and I didn't see what it was and I didn't ask either. I was just really glad that I could borrow her computer sometimes, and it wasn't that often either, but sometimes I borrowed it and I didn't really need the password because I didn't use her computer when she wasn't at home. It was just that later that evening, when Ida came and wanted to check something on the internet, I saw Frida lean over and whisper the password to her. And I don't know why it made me feel uneasy, and it wasn't exactly something that should make you feel uneasy, and it wasn't my business who she gave her password to, was it, and I sat there under the skylight and smoked and read through the assessments for the last time.

It was below freezing and icy and we'd finished our assessments and handed them in and bought wine and Ida came up and had some crap music with her that she put on and it was good to have some wine because it was a bit tense otherwise and I couldn't shake it off somehow. Later we went down to the college bar and sat there and there was some band playing and Frida was tired and had a sore tummy and had obviously thrown up that morning and wanted to go home soon but Ida and I didn't want to go home. Frida sat there and wanted to go home but she didn't go home, just sat there with us until they closed, and was tired and didn't say anything.

In the morning I ran down to the shop to buy some cigs and Mrs Landlord was standing there as usual and I said Jesus it's almost like winter down here, I said, and she nodded, and I don't know, but she didn't say anything, just stood there with her back to me putting things on the shelves. I had no intention of standing there and annoying her if she was in a bad mood, so I went out and had a smoke and froze out the back.

We got our assessments back after a few weeks and I didn't think I was going to get an A but I did and I mean, I never got good marks at school but now I'd got an A in red at the bottom of the page and I kind of wanted to ring Dad, y'know, but I couldn't bring myself to call because I didn't have much to say to him really, I thought. But of course I was happy about my A, I mean even though Frida had only got a B, and anyway it doesn't really matter what you get, I told her, it's all down to luck and what question they set, isn't it, I said, because Frida sat there without saying anything.

I don't know, I'd started to be all nervy and that, and I jumped when she said something or she moved and clattered about, and it was really great that she'd started to go home at the weekends and was away, because I had the whole flat to myself and could wander around and breathe, and I kind of stopped the minute she came home and I heard the key in the lock. And we were only going to keep the flat until the summer, so it wasn't that much longer. And later I said to Frida that it must be about time to give notice that we're moving out of the flat at the end of May. But then her dad was going to give notice for some reason. I don't know why, but he was going to do it, and I thought we could easily do it ourselves. But if her dad wanted to help then I should let him, she said. He's just being nice and trying to help out, she said, and of course he fucking can if that's what he wants, I said, it's nothing to get stroppy about, is it?

It was morning and she'd gone home for the weekend and I stood there and was about to make some coffee but I couldn't find the coffee filter cone, which usually hung there but it wasn't there now and wasn't anywhere else either, and I had no idea where it could be because I couldn't find it anywhere. I ran down and bought some instant coffee instead.

I then noticed later that the candlestick on the window sill had gone and I couldn't find the oven gloves anywhere. And she didn't drink coffee so she didn't need the filter cone but I did.

When she came back late on the Monday she'd apparently been to the doctor and she had gastritis and had got medicine for it. She put the jar of pills on the kitchen table and sat down to read and I didn't say anything about the things that were missing and I stirred my instant coffee and used a tea towel as an oven glove and put a candle in an old wine bottle.

And it was the end of the month and I don't know, but I just felt like I wanted to pay my part of the rent myself this time and I told her and she stared up at me from behind her glasses and said that she'd already fixed it with her dad so I couldn't just pay it myself whenever I felt like it. You're always being difficult, she said, and of course she could have the rent if that's how it was, and I didn't want to fight either, and there was a weird atmosphere, and even though we sat there opposite each other every evening and chatted, it wasn't the same as before. I ran down to get the money for her and popped into the shop to buy some cigs and there was Mrs Landlord and she was pissed off because she'd started to be like that and I don't know, she hardly said anything, just disappeared between the shelves. I told Frida when I got up to the flat that she's really grumpy these days, the woman in the shop, I said, and Frida looked down at the book she was reading and said she'd always been like that. Anyway it wasn't as easy to just nip down for some cigs anymore.

I watched her undress in the evening over there in her corner, with her short fat legs and small feet that were so heavy on the floor. And she lay in bed reading and I couldn't read or revise, I couldn't do anything around her anymore. I lay in bed and listened to her breathing and saw her body lying there under the covers.

And in the morning I was woken by her walking across the floor and clattering around in the kitchenette. I sat down opposite her at the kitchen table and she tensed and looked at the paper and wondered if I'd slept well and hasn't your dad called yet, she asked, and I looked at her mouth and the words it was forming. And the lock on the front door is difficult and stiff and I called the landlords about it yesterday but they haven't come and fixed the lock yet. Call them again then, she said, and turned the page of the paper and I nodded and said it's just you feel like a bit of a nag, don't you. She opened the jar of pills and swallowed one and I looked at her and she looked down at the newspaper. It's living with you that does for my stomach, she said, and turned the page and I looked at her. So it's me, you think that it's me, I said, and she turned the page. But it's us, isn't it, really, it's the two of us that don't work together, I said, and she got up and put her plate in the sink and walked with her heavy feet over to the toilet and closed the door. And I sat down under the skylight and opened it and pulled out a cigarette with trembling fingers. And she was in the toilet and soon I would hear her unlock the door and open it and soon, at any moment, the door handle would creak and she would come out again and fill everything with her silence and her heavy steps and I sat there and smoked and waited and trembled. And then she came out. I hate being here, she said. Right, I said, but there's only two months left.

I sat in the backyard and smoked and looked at the bulbs that were coming up, and it was only two months until the end of the contract and then we'd move and I didn't know where I was going to live but I wasn't going to live here, that's for sure. I popped into the shop and reminded Mrs Landlord about the lock, which is really stiff and you can hardly lock it, I said, and she didn't look at me, just nodded and disappeared into the back. And I watched her go, then I left. I sat in the park on some bench and the geese came over immediately, and I flicked my cigarette stub at them, and there was something uneasy about everything and I couldn't put my finger on it or understand it or figure it out.

She went home again at the weekend. And I don't know, but things kept on disappearing the whole time, small things kept disappearing, the colander and the whisk. I whipped things with a fork instead and kept the lid on the pan when I poured the water off the pasta, so it wasn't that big a deal and I didn't say anything about it. Every time she went home for the weekend things disappeared and I went around looking for them. And obviously we weren't going to be living there much longer, but they'd come with the trailer soon enough and take all the stuff, so she didn't need to take things with her now, but her things kind of diminished in numbers and vanished.

A few weekends later her dad was obviously going to come by and collect her, so I went into town and hung out and sat in the park and waited until they'd gone. And when I got in I saw straightaway that the lamp by my bed had been taken. I stood in the doorway and stared at the spot where the lamp had been and then I went to look and see if she'd put it somewhere else, but it was so fucking gone. And obviously I could sit at the kitchen table and study but I couldn't see why the bedside lamp was such a problem. I sat under the skylight and had a smoke and felt bad, and if only there had been someone I could call, but I didn't know anyone and I didn't want to talk to Ida about it either, and it wasn't something I could ring my dad about, and I wasn't in the mood to phone him anyway, but just felt fucking empty and I sat there smoking. And I couldn't let go of the lamp, because they knew I needed it to study, they knew that. She had started to empty the flat of things so that I wouldn't touch them.

I sat under the skylight and read because it was light until eight, and then I lit some candles and put them in bottles round about.

One of the landlords finally came up later on Friday to look at the lock and Frida had gone home for the weekend, so there I was sitting in the cold flat and smoking out the window, and he was nice, the landlord, standing there and sorting out the lock, and I sat by the window and smoked and he was a fireman as well. Cool job, I said, and he shrugged and carried on with the lock and I said that I wouldn't dare be a fireman or anything like that, even though I wanted to when I was little, I said, and smoked and he unscrewed the lock. Nice weather down here now, isn't it, not like up at my dad's where there's still snow, I said, and I don't know, but I'd got so kind of nervous recently, really fucking tense. I sat there and smoked and was tense and he didn't say anything and he was wasn't normally quiet but he was quiet now, and he stood there and didn't say anything and carried on with the lock and took it to pieces. I blew the smoke out through the window and he stood up straight and looked out of the window. Then he looked back down again and carried on with the lock. Dad usually hides the Easter eggs in the snow up at ours, and you have to go out and look for them, but there's no snow here now and there hasn't really been any, I said, and I don't know, I just sat there and he said nothing. I stubbed out my cigarette and lit a new one, and my hands were shaking and the smoke stung my eyes and he stood up and looked at me. We haven't had any rent for five months now, he said. What, I said, and I looked at him and he looked at me. You must have, I said, and smiled and took a drag on the cigarette, you have got the rent, haven't you, I said, and stood up. We've paid the rent, I've certainly given the rent to Frida every month. I looked at him and I didn't have a voice. I don't know. Have you not got the rent, I whispered, and he shook his head and there was something else that I didn't know, and he stood there and said there was something else I didn't know, and that I should know. I looked at him and his arms and hands were strong and his hands were so big and broad, if only I could hold them. I sat down by the window and looked out at the garden, and Frida's dad, he hadn't paid the rent because he wanted it to be lowered. But we don't want to lower the rent, he said, and I don't want you to either, I said. I didn't think it was too high. Well, said the landlord, but we'll have to go to court if we don't get the rent, and it's you and Frida who signed the contract. But I've paid, I said. I'm sure you did, he said, but we haven't had any rent.

He was finished with the lock and I sat by the window and watched him go. I walked backwards and forwards across the floor and then when I was in the middle of a lap the phone rang and I picked it up and it was Ida. I had been about to phone Dad but it was Friday so he'd be at the pizza place as usual and now Ida had phoned and I went down to meet her at the college bar instead. And Ida wondered what was up but I didn't know how to say that it was fucking everything and it was difficult to say anything about it really. Oh I don't know, I said, and drank my beer and felt cold. She cadged a cigarette from me and lit up, and I said it looked like I'd need to find somewhere else to live. But there's only a month left, she said. Yes, I said, but a month can be a bloody long time, can't it, I said, and she looked at me and drew on the cigarette and nodded. Of course I understand, she said, come and stay with me then, why don't you, she said, and I don't know, there was this fucking uneasiness everywhere and it was making me cold and she sat there and said I could go and live with her, she said, and there was nothing I would rather do. So you mean it then, I said, and my fingers were trembling, holding on to my fag, and she said of course I bloody mean it, you should come and stay with me.

I packed my things on the Monday and dragged them with me on the bus over to Ida's, and she had a big student room and had sorted out a mattress on the floor for me. Then I went back to the attic and got some more things and waited for Frida, and I don't know, I was sitting under the skylight smoking when I heard her put the key in the lock. She pushed open the door and I said nothing, I looked at her and sat there freezing and smoking, and didn't know what to say to her, I'd been so fucking angry all weekend, gone around being so fucking angry, but I wasn't angry now, only sat there shaking and was just fucking exhausted. And now when I was going to open my mouth I had no voice. The landlord was here, I said, and she jumped and started to rummage around in her bag. What have you done, you've been lying to me, you lied to me, I said, and she made staccato moves around the room and unpacked her things or whatever, moved her things, and I was dry in the mouth and had no words, nothing. You've been lying to me all the time, you lied, I whispered, and there was no anger left. I got up and put on my shoes and she stood in the room with her back to me. I picked up the boxes that I'd packed and opened the door and walked out. Down in the backyard I turned and looked up at the window in the gable and she was standing there.

I dreaded cleaning and emptying the flat for the whole month. I lay there on Ida's mattress and revised for my last exam and sat with the others down in the kitchen and ate pasta. But then it was the end of the month and of course I was going to go there and clean and empty the flat, after all, I'd borrowed all the things and hadn't had to pay for them.

We barely said a word to each other, Frida and me. Just stood there and washed the windows and the floor, but she was nice and said all the right things and I got nervous and couldn't answer, and I didn't know what to do with her questions and words that, well, kind of had something more behind them. Then later her dad came with the car and the trailer behind it. He came up the stairs and I heard his feet on the stairs and he came into the room, short and grey, stood in the room with his face and not a smile to be seen. And he told us what to carry, and it was fucking heavy carrying those beds down the winding stairs, and he took one end and I took the other and Frida ran up and down with small things, and he and I manoeuvred and carried the beds and the table and it was no skin off my nose to carry heavy things, I was used to that from home, but I couldn't help thinking that it grated all the same that me and her dad were twisting and levering the beds and our backs on the narrow stairs and Frida was carrying a lamp. And no one said a word, fucking silence.

My things were standing in a corner and the trailer was full and ready. I stood in the backyard and Frida's dad closed the trailer. Frida got into the passenger seat and closed the door and he got in beside her and they sat there side by side in the car and he started the engine.

I ran up the stairs and my back hurt and my hands, but I was so fucking relieved and I sat under the skylight and had a smoke. Then I hauled my things down into the backyard and went into the shop with the keys and handed them back and I'd heard from the landlord that they were in negotiations and he didn't know yet whether we would need to go to court.

Then later I sat there on the platform and smoked while I waited for the train back to my dad's where I was going to stay for the summer, and I'd told him, and he hadn't said anything. I sat there with all my things around me, a shit-load of things and the stereo.

It was in the middle of the summer that I got some papers through the post to say that I'd have to appear in the county court one day in September because there was to be a settlement or something like that, I don't know. Then I got a letter from Frida's dad saying that they could remove me from the contract completely so that I didn't have to go and Frida could be responsible for everything because, as it was now, we were both responsible for what her dad had done. And I didn't know what to do, and I sat there at my dad's kitchen table and read the letter and crumpled up the envelope and threw it into the wood box, and I wasn't going to let them remove me from the contract, because my name was there and it had been there all the time, even though they hadn't wanted it to be. But more letters came, really bloody nice letters from Frida, wondering how I was getting on with my dad and all that, and if I just signed some papers I wouldn't need to go down for the court hearing. But it was a bit late to drop it, and I didn't want to do what they wanted me to, anyway. I realised it wasn't for my sake that they wanted to do it, but that the rent was lying in a pot somewhere and they were going to negotiate about it, and there might be money for us if the landlords didn't get it all, like they should, and they'd taught me that behind every word is something else you have to understand and grasp. Of course, I could have given the money to Frida's dad, but I didn't want to give anything of mine anymore. I threw my cigarette butt into the wood box and phoned Ida and asked if I could stay with her in Malmö in September. Of course you can, that would be so cool, she said, and I grinned and looked out of the window at Dad who was trundling up the hill on the moped and had obviously been shopping.

I sat on the train down to Malmö, and the courthouse wasn't actually in the town but in the next county, and I sat on the bus out there and felt that uneasiness again.

It was an old stone building with climbing ivy and I went up the steps into an enormous echoing hall with pillars and stone benches. The landlords were sitting there and said hello, and Frida and her dad were standing there and her dad didn't even manage a smile, but Frida, she twisted her mouth and asked how I was, and what was it like living at home with Dad again, and I don't know, I didn't manage to squeeze any kind of answer out but just froze and sat down on a bench. The landlords sat there, chatting and rustling their papers, and Frida and her dad stood by the window and mumbled, and I sat there freezing and had started to shake again.

The strawberry blond judge weighed down one end of the large oak table, and the clerk sat next to the judge, and the landlords sat next to each other and Frida and her father and me, and it was autumn outside. And the judge gave permission to speak and wanted to hear everyone's statements about what had happened and everyone had their turn, and the landlords said that they hadn't got any rent for five months and they didn't want to lower the rent on the flat as it was as good as newly decorated, they thought, and then it was Frida's turn to say what had happened but she didn't need to say much because her dad was sitting there and took over, and he thought the rent was too high and then there was the furniture that I had used and exploited and they felt they'd been exploited by me. Then it was my turn to give a statement and I sat there shaking and I didn't know what to say either and there was silence round the table and there I sat, and started to tell and explain, then hesitated and stopped, and in the silence I heard Frida's dad, I heard him whisper to Frida, look at her, he hissed, and turned towards me in his chair, look at her. And I looked at the judge and the judge looked back and winked at me and I carried on and the judge looked at me and nodded and listened and I looked at his hands, fat red hairy hands that were on the table. And I had paid the rent every month to Frida, I said, and I didn't think the rent was too high and I didn't want it lowered, the flat was really nice, I said. And then the judge said to Frida's dad that what he had done was illegal, to do something in someone else's name, so I could sue him if I wanted to, the judge said and the corners of Frida's dad's mouth tightened.

I sat out in the hall for some bits and waited on the cold stone bench, and sometimes I sat in with the judge and the clerk by the large oak table, and the judge was finding it hard to get enough air and he sighed and breathed heavily. And then I had to sit out in the hall again, and it was cold and the landlords and Frida and her father were there, and no one had any words to say, and our steps echoed, and I sat and ate my packed lunch, and outside the day was fading into evening.

By the time we reached a settlement the evening had almost turned to night. And we sat there at the oak table again, all of us, to divide up the money, and the landlords got most of it but they wanted it all. Frida and I got the rest, a few thousand each. But I gave a thousand to Frida's dad for the hire of the furniture, so Frida and her dad got several thousand, but then he had to pay the rent for June because he hadn't given notice on the flat like he was supposed to, so he only had a thousand left after that. Frida and her dad sat there with a thousand and her dad was pale and rigid.

And it was Frida's dad who had collected the rent and kept the money, so he had to write out the cheques. And tomorrow you must go to the bank and withdraw the money and make sure it's not fake, the judge said, and gave me the cheque. Because he knew all about things like that and was suspicious of people and now I had to learn that too.

Then everything was sorted, and I stood there and shook hands with everyone, the judge's large red hands, and there was Frida's dad shaking hands with the landlords, but he didn't even try to take my hand. I held out my hand and he looked away and then took it limply and dropped it.

I watched Frida walk away with her father. They walked side by side, her blonde ponytail and his pale grey scalp. I sat freezing on the stone bench and the buses had stopped running into Malmö. The judge locked the doors and set the alarm and it was night and somewhere in it Ida was waiting. And the judge waved me over and I walked down the courthouse steps with the judge and the judge wasn't going into Malmö and it took a couple of hours but he drove me. I sat there beside him in the car, and it was warm and smelt faintly of aftershave, and he sat beside me, big, with his red hairy hands on the wheel, he sat breathing and sighing and he'd never been involved in such long negotiations, nine hours. He sighed and drove and I sat beside him and dozed.

Four Hundred Kronor

HER COAT SWUNG round her legs as she walked and finally it felt a bit like spring and there was a gurgling from the gutters and she picked her way along the icy roads and pavements and slipped every now and then. She caught glimpses of herself in the shop windows, her handbag gleaming and the hand that held it hard. And she hadn't grown up here in the city but she lived in the city now, and studied here and had piles of books at home that she read, sat and read for several hours a day, and went for a walk every so often. She swept back her hair and her heels slipped on the ice and the sun swept over the city and the snow and the slush that she stepped carefully over and she couldn't be late so that Hans would have to wait for her today because Hans was coming, and she wanted to buy something nice for the evening when Hans was coming, and she didn't know Hans that well yet so she didn't know what he liked, but they would have to buy something good for the evening and she couldn't eat whatever either because you had to be careful with what you ate and filled your body with and where the food came from, and he thought she was spartan, he had said, but she wasn't really that spartan. And maybe he would stay over again this time, she thought, like the last time, and she had washed herself carefully in the morning and maybe she could have a child with Hans, she thought, and she hadn't thought about having a child before, but with Hans she did because he was an architect, Hans, and it was a proper profession he had and he worked as an architect and there was something calm about him, he was so calm, and an education, he had an education. And she had said to Hans when they met that he should know that she was studying and that she was serious, and she left the books lying around when he came, the books were piled on her desk where she had left them, but he hadn't said anything about them. She had tidied away a whole load of things when he came so there was space and not lots of things lying around everywhere, and she had left out the books, but he barely looked at them. And then, when he was at her place the last time, he had looked in the cupboards and she had said that he couldn't just look in her cupboards like that but he had laughed and teased and looked in them and she hadn't tidied the cupboards and what have you got to hide, he had said, but she wasn't trying to hide anything, and after all he was the one looking, what are you looking for, she asked, and he laughed and even though she had tidied and put things away he found things and asked about them and she sat and answered and got all stiff and he said you don't need to be like that, he said, because it was just that he was curious about her and wanted to know things and wanted to know everything, but you can't get to know everything about someone in one go, she said. And now she could see him standing by the park benches up ahead, waiting, but she reckoned she wasn't late and she looked at the church clock and saw that she wasn't late so he must have been a bit early and he waved and she didn't really think she could wave back in front of everyone, so she walked faster and her heels slipped on the ice and there was salt sprinkled everywhere, and there he was standing, waving, and she smiled and he wanted to hug her, stand there and hug. He let go of her and she straightened her hair and she hadn't had time to dry clean her coat yet, she was wearing a dirty coat, and he must have been able to smell it and it was obvious that she should have cleaned it. He looked at her and stroked her hair and she started to walk and he walked with her because now they were going to buy something good for the evening, and they hadn't gone shopping together many times before, but now they were going to the shop to buy some stuff, and Hans held the shopping basket and she went and lingered by the shelves and pushed her hair out of her face and then she saw him.

He was standing there rocking and she'd known that she was going to bump into him and she looked at his neck and hair that hung down around it, fair and greasy. He was wearing green army trousers and you could smell him from way off, his stink. He didn't live in the city but had somewhere outside town, and now he had obviously come into town, and he couldn't have known she lived around here because she hadn't said, because then he'd be ringing on her doorbell all the time, wanting to come in. He stood there, twitching a bit and rocking, and she backed her way round behind the shelves and hid, and picked something up and read it, and Hans wondered what was wrong, but it was nothing. She pushed back her hair and she didn't eat meat but we could have salmon, she said, and he said he would like that and her fingers trembled through her hair and if she waited a bit he would have left by then, so she dawdled around in the shop, waiting, and Hans dawdled with her. But we should maybe go and stand in the queue, Hans said, because there was a long queue and they got in line and she could tell where he was by the smell, can you smell that, Hans said, and she nodded. It must be someone in the queue, he said, and she nodded and heard his laugh towards the front of the queue where he was laughing and she pushed her hair back and the queue was practically at a standstill and Hans went forwards to have a look and it's that druggie, he said to her, he's probably got no money, Hans said, that druggie, you can smell him from here, he said, and she heard the girl at the till talking to him because he didn't have enough money, she went up on her toes and saw him standing there by the till, grinning, with the snus oozing down his teeth and his cheekbones pushing against his skin and he grinned and stood there rocking and didn't have enough money and the queue stood still and sighed and heaved and looked at their watches and she opened her handbag and took out a hundred kronor note and handed it to Hans and said you go and give it to him, she said, and her hand was shaking and Hans said are you going to give that to that druggie, he said, and she nodded and you can see that he's not a drug addict, she said. It's obvious he's a junkie, he said, and she held out the money and said you can go and give it to him, she said, and he hissed go and give it to the druggie yourself, and she felt her mouth tighten and you can see that he's not a drug addict, she said, can't you tell the difference between people, she said. He looked at her and said nothing. Then he took the hundred kronor and went to the till at the front of the queue where he was standing and rocking and grinning and didn't have enough money. Jesus, thanks, she heard him say to Hans, and she leant out and saw him stand up there by the till and grin and wipe his arm over his mouth. Jesus Christ, thanks mate, he stood grinning and rocking, fucking thanks, he shouted at Hans and Hans had walked back and was standing beside her and hissed that it was a good thing he could buy his cigarettes now and really great that he was standing over there shouting and he started to light up a fag and she saw one of the staff push him out. So you give money to druggies to buy cigarettes, Hans said, and she pushed back her hair and said that he could buy what he wanted with the money. A hundred kronor, he said, and she saw that there was a salt mark on her leather boots. You could see that he wasn't a drug addict, she said, and looked at her boots and rummaged around in her bag for some paper to dry it off, that wasn't a drug addict, couldn't you tell, she said, and Hans said it's obvious he was a junkie, he was all twitchy, you must've seen that, and you didn't get as close, he said. That's the side effects of the medicine, she said, surely you could tell it was side effects, she said. Let's go home now, he said, and she nodded and he wanted to pay for the food but obviously they were going to split it. And she hadn't seen him for a few years now, maybe. She wasn't sure. But she couldn't be seeing him all the time, she didn't want to, though he did ring sometimes, got it into his mind to ring, several times a day he might call, and she didn't answer but let it just ring and sat there and studied and tried to read even though he kept ringing, and now when she hadn't seen him for ages, she'd just seen him again. She walked beside Hans and he held her hand and the bag in the other and it wasn't exactly sunny but sometimes the sun came out and the ice had started to melt, and she stepped carefully over the puddles and snow and she had a recipe for salmon with chilli and lime if he'd like that, she said, and he nodded and held her hand and she pushed her hair back and maybe he would stay over again like the last time, lie there beside her all night. She hadn't been able to sleep when he was lying so close beside her, but had gone numb, up-close to him, lay warm and numb. She lifted her feet carefully on the ice and then suddenly he was coming straight towards them and the smell. You thought I didn't see you, didn't you, he grinned with his grey teeth, he hadn't had teeth like that before, had always been careful with our teeth at home, but now his teeth were grey with plaque in between. Huh, you thought I didn't see you, he said, and she looked at him and felt her face and the roots of her hair get hot because she had seen him after all. Of course I saw you, he said, but you pretended not to see me, he grinned. I saw you when you came in, he said, and she nodded and he had seen her the whole time, he had seen her. Do you want money, she said, and he grinned. You thought I hadn't seen you, didn't you, he said, and she rummaged around in her handbag. Right, because you didn't want to see me, he said, and stood there rocking. And Dad, right, he came to see me recently, he said, and rocked and he had one hand knotted behind his back. So you should be able to do it too, come and say hello, you should, he said, and she nodded and opened her wallet and took out three hundred kronor and gave it him and he grinned and took the money and the hand that took it was dirty with nails that were split and black. We're in a hurry, she said, and he stood with the money and waved it around and rocked backwards and forwards and she closed her bag and pushed back her hair and said we've got to be going now, she said, and he grinned and waved the money around. Put it in your pocket, she said, and started to cross the puddles and ice and he stood and grinned and shouted after her that you thought I hadn't seen you and were hiding away, weren't you, he shouted after her. She slipped in her heels on the ice and Hans was behind her and caught her by the arm and the tears started to spill over and it was stupid that they were doing that, that they had started to run.

Norrgården

THE FARM STOOD there and looked out over the water with its old windows. I drove the car around to the earth cellar and Tobias was wrapped in his silence, a silence that had crept up and settled around him, meaning he must be hungry. It was the new low building on the right that we were going to stay in, and the key was hanging on the nail under the step as it should. Some artists were supposed to be staying over there in the old building opposite but there was no sign of any artists, just some boots on the barn bridge[2] and beer cans and umbrellas. Tobias got our stuff and put it on the grass and it was a nice old farm that stood there, just stood there, and had done for a really long time. I went up onto the glass-panelled veranda and looked out over the water and down across the meadow and suddenly I saw that there were things in the grass down there, everywhere, and it must've been the artists who'd set out the knotted roots and branches that they'd painted, and something leathery that was hanging between two posts. I don't know anything about art, really, but I'm sure it's some sort of art, I said to Tobias, who was carrying in the bags. So they'd obviously got something done already, the artists, and were exhibiting it so it could be seen from the road, even though there didn't seem to be many cars on the road, but some must come by.

Later we sat and ate in the kitchen and I noticed that there was a light in one of the windows, over there in the

2. A common feature of Scandinavian barns, which are often arranged over two storeys. The 'barn bridge' is an external ramp leading to the upper floor, providing access for vehicles to drive in the hay.

old building where the artists were, so they must have come back, and of course we should have gone over and said hello but we just sat there, and we couldn't see anything outside because it had become dark and it was black, because it was August after all. Tobias made his way to the outside toilet up in the woods with a torch. I could see him through the kitchen window, stumbling over roots, the torch flickering. I was used to these parts, and the dark here, but Tobias had grown up with street lights outside his window so it must have been bright as day all the time.

There was only a cold water tap in the kitchen so I had to heat a large pan of water and Tobias stood there and washed himself and I lay in bed and read and I heard someone walking outside. I should maybe have closed the curtains but I didn't think that anyone would be walking around out there, did I, and you couldn't see anything outside, but you could see everything inside, and there I was, lying there, all visible, and I kind of froze and lay there listening. Tobias was busy with the bowl out there in the kitchen, and poured out the water, and then I heard steps outside, heard them disappearing into the distance.

Tobias fell asleep straightaway and I lay there and listened to his breathing and the house, which creaked and groaned a bit.

The gravel track wound its way into the forest and I was driving and Tobias was sitting with the map on his knees. There was some silence going on again, and the forest stood tall and dark as it should, and always had done, and every now and then, in the middle of the forest, was a small cottage huddling among the midges and dark, and they were probably hunting cabins because no one would actually want to live there.

We drove down to the tarn and I laid out the towels on the marsh grass and the water lilies lay floating, their white crowns swaying, and the water was warm now in August and the dragonflies hovered over it. And he sat down on a towel and ate sandwiches while I slipped into the water and he had his silence and he was good at that, at staying silent for a really long time. He could sit there and be silent because he was happy in his silence, sat there brooding, and it was midgey and the midges, they loved me, and there were probably some midges up by him, too, but as soon as they caught sight of me they came over singing and looking for space.

When we drove back to the farm afterwards, the artists were sitting there on the barn bridge, drinking beer amongst all the boots, so obviously artists can sit and drink beer and get tipsy in the middle of the day and then carry on painting later, I suppose. We should really go and say hello now, and it's not that it made me nervous, but it was strange in a way, all the same. Linn stood there small and thin and held out her hand to take mine and she had a damp, limp hand that I tried to grasp, and her hair hung down her back and was tangled and thick, and Mickel sat on the step with a can of beer in his hand, and I mean, he could've put it down and shook my hand, but he didn't. He just looked at me and I, well, looked away, because I didn't dare look at him, but could maybe have a peek later instead, because he had a grey and scarred face and walked around with it in the summer light and his eyes burned out from it. And I was uncomfortable as well, I think, because I remembered that I'd been lying in bed the night before and he'd seen me. Tobias had his silence and stood and was silent and Linn disappeared inside to get something. Mickel grinned and raised his beer and took a swig and the silence stood and swayed and Mickel scratched himself, leisurely scratched himself somewhere on the back of his neck, and then got up, and he was tall and thin and sort of bowlegged. He stood there with his bow legs and grinned over at the meadow. So you're academics are you, he said, and took another swig of beer from the can and I stood there and looked at him and Tobias did the same and Mickel grinned at the meadow. Then Linn came out again and had cigarettes with her and asked if we'd seen Mickel's art down there in the meadow. You should go down and have a look at his work, Linn said, and Mickel took a cigarette and lit it and said I suppose you don't smoke, and I shook my head and said that depends on how you define academics, because obviously we were, but Tobias, I said, he's actually a musician and you're not really an academic, are you, I said to Tobias, so it depends on what you mean, obviously, I said, because Tobias went to a folk high school[3], but I'm an academic, I guess that's what I am, though I would never really have thought that before, I said, and laughed. And Linn smoked and picked her toenails and Mickel grinned and drank and looked at the meadow.

In the evening the rain came, and I stood on the veranda and listened to it splash and pour down into the barrel on the corner and the outside lamp flickered in the rain and dark. I stumbled up into the woods with the umbrella and sat down on one of the toilets and leant the torch up against the wall and read something old and yellow that was lying there. Then I heard steps out there, and the rattling of the hook on the toilet next door, so one of them was sitting there, and there was only a plank wall between us, where the wasps had built a nest. The rain pattered on the metal roof of the toilet, and the other person sat there and was silent, and I listened for sounds but heard nothing. And when I left the toilet I saw there was a light on in there, a faint light, so there was someone sitting there with a torch, just sitting.

And in the middle of the night I woke up and sat bolt upright because there was something, and I looked at Tobias and he was lying there looking at me, and what are you lying there looking at, I said. Did you hear something, he said, and I don't know if I heard anything in particular, but there had been a sound. Of course there are strange sounds in houses like this, I said.

3. Adult education institutes in Scandinavia that provide practical courses rather than academic qualifications.

It was dinner time and we were sitting at the kitchen table eating when he suddenly appeared at the kitchen door and scratched his backside. I jumped, as I was totally bloody unprepared, and he grinned and said that here in the country you don't knock, and I sat at the table and Tobias was sitting opposite. I don't suppose you have any wine you could lend us, he said, not that he'd thought of asking, but Linn thought I should, even though you probably don't drink wine, and if you did have any, you probably wouldn't want to give it to us anyway, he said, and grinned, and it was as if his mouth was just a bit twitchy and askew. I got up and said of course we had wine and would be happy to give it to them. And he looked around with those squinty eyes of his that burned. Anyway, we can drive over and get more from the supermarket on Monday, can't we, I said to Tobias, nothing difficult about that, I said, and asked if he'd like red or white and he said that he'd take whatever as long as it was wine and we were happy to give it to him because he hadn't thought we would. Tobias sat chewing, and there was silence in the kitchen, and I handed the wine bottle to Mickel and he disappeared, disappeared really quietly, and I walked around the kitchen, and I was calm, of course I was, and it wasn't anything to be worried about, but I should have locked the door maybe, I don't know, because out here in the country, people just walk in. We're in the country now, you see, I said to Tobias, and here you don't lock your door or knock. Tobias nodded and sat there chewing and I walked around the kitchen backwards and forwards and Tobias, he sat there eating and obviously had an appetite and kept eating.

It was still raining the next day and it was cold on the veranda, just sitting there, but I wrapped myself up in some blankets and sat there and drank tea and read and I saw that Mickel had some project on the go out there in the rain. He was out there, building something, hammering, and I don't know. Thin and bowlegged, he stood there and the rain poured off him. He'd obviously found an old sou'wester somewhere that he'd put on, and if there had been a kitchen door it would have been good, not that I had any problems with going past him, but all the same. I didn't dread it either, walking past him, but I'd been needing the loo for a while now, and had held on and put it off because he'd go in soon, I mean stop and take a break. In the end I went out all the same and stood there on the step with my umbrella, and he didn't hear me or see me, just carried on hammering in nails, and I should've maybe said something but I didn't know what so I walked slowly over the grass and didn't want to disturb him and I crept up into the woods and slipped with my boots on the wet roots and dusk was falling and I hadn't noticed before, but now I saw that there was a dead elk lying in the nettles by the toilet and it stank, the grass growing up through the skull. I should probably ring the agents and tell them about the dead elk and it was really horrible of the hunters to just leave it like that on the property. I could have gone out through the window at the back of the house, I realised, but I certainly bloody wasn't going to sneak around like that and crouch down. I was going to walk in through my own bloody door. And he wasn't there anymore when I went back, and I stamped over the grass in my boots and up the steps and looked all around, and it was some kind of installation he was building from those old hay poles he'd found, and it smelt of cigarette smoke so he was there, somewhere, I just couldn't see him, probably sitting on the veranda smoking. Oh, I don't know, sneaking around like that, I said to Tobias when I got in, I mean, we have just as much right to stay here as him. I'm not sneaking around, he said, and of course he bloody didn't, he just sat there in his bloody silence. You're always happy enough in there somewhere, I said, and Tobias put some snus in under his lip and sat down and sucked on it, and he put things in his mouth all the time but nothing came out, and bloody well take that snus out now, I shouted, and he wondered what the fuck was wrong with me. I don't know, maybe it was a strange thing to say. I went into the kitchen and it was dark now and you couldn't see anything outside, so you were completely bloody closed in. I went out into the bedroom and turned off the light and looked over to the artists' house from behind the curtains, because there were lights on in there, but I didn't see anything. Bloody idiot, I said, and that put some wind into Tobias' sail, evidently, because he suddenly shouted something from the sitting room that I couldn't make out, but that he'd obviously been successful in formulating and managed to spit out, and that was bloody rare, I said, and he stood in the doorway and stared at me and I said, I don't know, he was overreacting or whatever, I said, and he shouted that if anyone was overreacting then it certainly wasn't him. No, I said, because you're as good as dead, and have been ever since spring sometime, and I don't know what happened, I said, and that got him going and he started to kick the chair, an antique chair, and everything was from the turn of the century, and that's some way to behave, kicking it to bits, I said. You'll have to mend it later, I said, and he kicked away, and he had shoes on inside because of the cold, so there wasn't much left of the chair, just a split and broken back, and it's people like you that lash out, I said, people like you who can't express themselves and get the words out of here, your mouth, I said, and pointed. This is where they're supposed to come out, see, but it seems like you can't get anything out so you kick lovely old chairs to pieces instead, and it's not even your chair, I said, and he had picked up a bit of the chair and was hitting the doorframe with it and shouting because he'd obviously found some words, and kept on repeating them. You'll make dents in the doorframe with that, so you better tell the agents about it later and pay for it, I don't know, compensation you know, pay for it, I said, and he wrenched open the outside door and grabbed a raincoat and disappeared out. I walked back and forth a few times and it wasn't that big a deal, really, and he'd be back soon I reckoned, and I'd been there before when he had a meltdown and it was good for him in a way, to get these things out, because he found it bloody hard otherwise.

So I sat down on the veranda and read and it was semi-dark outside and he would come back, and I mean I had other things to do than just wait for him. I went out to the loo and had a wander in the woods with the torch. It was one way of not walking straight into the dead elk, lying there on the ground, which had been lying there for ages. It stank and the skull shone white in the dark. I took hold of some bones and tried to drag it down onto the grass because I was going to ring the agents about it, I thought. It was heavy as hell, though it was only a small elk, or perhaps even a calf, and maybe I'd manage to get it at least some way onto the grass and leave it outside the barn doors.

I lay on the big box bed that creaked the moment you moved and I couldn't lock the door either, because then he couldn't get in, and it was quiet but with lots of noises in the silence and I listened to them and it was probably mice in the attic, and I lay there all stiff in a corner of the bed and stared at the strip of light from the outside lamp that shone in under the blinds.

Later I heard him stomping on the veranda and prising off his shoes. He opened the door and I sat up and asked where he'd been keeping himself and he grinned and tripped over the sandals in the hall, and obviously he'd been down with the holiday people on the bend because they were having a party there, and he'd met some people on the road who dragged him down to the party. So he had sat there on their veranda and been given schnapps and sucked on some crayfish tails and this guy called Bosse was there with an accordion and some Sophie girl. How do you mean, some Sophie girl, I said. The one that's always riding past here, he slurred, and had obviously had a fine old time, sitting there and enjoying himself.

It rained the next day too, and I turned the dial on the radio and tried to find a station with the weather to hear about the rain and how long it would last, and Tobias had been out to the outhouse and found some old wood glue and had sat on the veranda and glued the chair back together and was sanding it now, and fucking hell, he'd said when he came in, there's a bloody dead animal outside the barn that they've obviously dragged down. But it was me who'd dragged it down, wasn't it, or should it just be left lying up there in the woods, rotting, and I guess we'd better bury it or something, I said. Well we can't leave it there, in front of the barn, stinking and frightening the life out of people, he said. But a rotten elk isn't really much to keep, or much to be frightened of, obviously.

And there was going to be a surströmming[4] party at the Albertssons, which he'd obviously heard about from the holidaymakers, so we were invited and we should take the artists with us, they'd told him, but I said they wouldn't eat rotten fish. Do you think Stockholmers eat that, I said and grinned, and even though he was a Stockholmer himself he agreed. Tobias ate anything, though. You're not discerning about what you put in your mouth, I said, and looked out at the yard because Mickel had got started again, out in the rain, and was obviously trying to prise whatever it was into the storehouse, and I don't know, it looked like some sort of guillotine or something, because artists, they can make anything.

At least it would be warm until Saturday and stop raining. Only, then the midges came out. The eggs had been lying in pools of spit in the warm forest hollows. I'd seen the pools and puddles heaving with larvae, and when the sun shone it took no time for them to hatch and crawl out, and there they came, humming from the woods, shimmering

4. A traditional Swedish dish of fermented herring.

and hungry, and I swore at them and Mickel sat there on the grass and grinned. He scratched the back of his neck and said that in Stockholm there weren't many midges, were there, he said, and why did I let myself be bothered by such a small thing? In the country, you know, he said and took a swig of beer, in the country, there's often midges, he said. And I knew that perfectly well, I'd grown up there after all, and I wasn't bothered by a few midges, exactly, but there were loads now, after the rain, I said. And of course, he wasn't bothered by the midges, because no one would want to sit on that bastard and suck. And he hadn't said anything about the elk, though it was obvious where it was lying, stinking in the sun, and Linn wouldn't go past the barn at all, but I said that they were going to come and bury it after the weekend. Mickel got up and tottered on his bowed legs and his eyes were glassy and red in his pale face, and we were going to the surströmming party so he'd better fold those legs of his into the car, and Linn was sitting on the step with a small mirror, putting on makeup, and she brushed her hair and sprayed perfume over the whole yard.

The Albertssons had put out the tables in the barn but we opened the cans outside so they wouldn't spray the wood. Couldn't get rid of it for years, I said, and everyone had been asked to bring their own, so I got the boxes out of the boot and put out the flatbread and beer, and the artists didn't have anything with them because they didn't have any money, and I'd said that we'd share what we had, I'd said, and Linn had said that it was nice that they were invited, and Mickel had grinned. But now he was sitting there by the table and smoking and had got a schnapps. He said that he didn't intend to eat anything, because it's really only Linn you invited. Of course I meant both of you, I said, but he obviously didn't believe it. He hadn't eaten fermented fish before, either, so Lena tried to show him how to cut open the belly and pull out the spine and clean it, and the Albertssons had schnapps that was passed round and there were songs and

I didn't drink schnapps normally but it was Saturday, after all, and it was good schnapps they were offering. And the Albertssons had children and relatives and the like who were sitting there and Tobias sat there as well and said nothing but people were used to that. He sat there and listened and took it all in and saved it, but he didn't say anything or take part or offer anything himself. Mickel sat there with a poker-straight back on the long bench and ate surströmming and was pale because he was eating and didn't have any potato or flat bread to go with it, even though Lena had showed him how to wrap it in the flat bread. Linn was eating sausages like the kids, and the Albertssons' schnapps was doing the rounds and the midges found their way in through the cracks in the door and they had plenty to choose from tonight.

Mickel sat up straight and downed his schnapps and his grin hovered and twitched and he had managed to eat five surströmming, he said, and looked to each side but no one commented on it. I saw him disentangle his legs from the bench after a while and head towards the toilet and we realised that he had something wrong with his guts, because sometimes he walked around bent double and sat there on the loo with a torch at night and moaned and pushed, and fermented fish could get your stomach moving quick, even if it didn't normally.

Tobias sat there and chewed, and had filled up his plate again even though the others had stopped, and I poured some more schnapps because they passed it to me, and I mean, it was bloody rare that I drank schnapps otherwise, and Mickel had come back and sat down again opposite and was smoking and looking around and I drank my schnapps and he could sit there grinning, for all I cared, without it bothering me, because I had other things to bother me than that bloody grin that was always on his face, or maybe it was his cheekbones that did it. The Albertsson children had disappeared and gone to bed and the Bosse guy was playing his accordion and I was going to drive back later, because

Tobias hadn't got it together to pass his driving test even though he'd been trying for several years, so it was me who was driving, but I mean it was the back of beyond and there had never been any police here. Mickel sat there smoking opposite me and said to Linn you wouldn't have thought we'd be invited, he said, and I caught a sneer and said of course we'd ask them, and this wasn't really that expensive anyway, I said, and Linn put on some lipgloss. But you didn't say hello the other day, he said, and I don't know, but of course it kind of put me on my guard and one of my legs started to sort of twitch. How do you mean, I said, and picked up my schnapps and was about to take a sip but the glass was empty so I would have to pour myself some more and it was bloody difficult to get the cork out and he grinned and said that the day before yesterday I was out there working in the yard when you went past without saying hello, that even though you walked right past me you didn't say hello. I don't know, living that close and not saying hello, he said, and I stared at his mouth, the way it moved, and my leg twitched away under the table, and I couldn't stop it, however hard I tried, and my foot jumped up and down and his cheekbones were, like, grinning, and he was enjoying something and was mulling on it, and I stared at him and he said that he had been standing out there in the rain, doing some woodwork, and you walked right past without saying anything so I didn't think that you'd invite us here, he said, and I stared at him, where he was sitting opposite me at the table. And Linn said that's enough Mickel, she said, and smiled at me and raised her glass and I sipped some schnapps but I didn't down it in one. And he sat there on the other side of the table with his skin stretched greyish yellow over his cheekbones and Linn smiled and said that's enough now Mickel, and Mickel grinned and looked to each side then lit a cigarette and sat there with his long crooked back and smoked and Tobias sat and ate apple pie and had his mouth full so he sat there chewing. Just walked straight past without saying hello, even though we're neighbours, Mickel said, and Linn nudged him in the ribs and I looked at him and stood up and I think I knocked something over, certainly seemed to, but I don't know, and stood there and pointed a finger at him, I had my finger on him, because there he sat, and I stood and pointed at him and everything was silent, not a sound, and I shouted and you, what about you then, I shouted, you didn't say hello either, you didn't say hello in the first place. It was bloody well you who didn't say hello, I shouted and pointed, it was you. He sat paralysed and I stretched over and blatantly poked him. Don't you understand it was you, I shouted, and he started to unravel his legs from the bench and said I won't talk to people like you, I won't. He stumbled towards the barn door and managed to open it and turned in the doorway and said you're exactly like my dad, he said, then left. There was total silence after that. I sat down and took another beer and Bosse got going and started playing again. Tobias sat there and thought that it was maybe time to go home now, all the same. Of course he wanted to go home, now that the food was finished, and of course I could drive, really slowly. I mean, of course I could drive.

Mickel wasn't anywhere to be seen anymore and Linn had been out to look for him and she thought we might as well go because he'll find his way, she said. I took the beer and went out to the car and tripped over someone's bike lying there in the grass, or, I don't know. I put the beer can between the seats and Linn crawled into the back and Tobias managed to say that I was to drive really bloody slowly because you can hardly walk, he said, but I said that driving and walking are two totally different things, aren't they, I said, and started the car and rolled down the hill and out onto the gravel track and I turned the lights to full beam because there were elks and things and they'd seen bears or something, but it wasn't a bloody bear walking up ahead it was a tall bastard walking on two legs and swaying. There he was, walking in the full beam and seeing nothing. I saw him, and I slowed down and stopped because to walk on foot, it was at least ten kilometres or something. But Linn sat in the back and she thought I should just drive on because he's walking, she said, he wants to walk. I rolled down the window and slowed down and stopped and said did he want to hop in? But he didn't bloody stop, he just kept walking with his pale bloody skin stretched tight over his cheek bones. Come on, you should get in, I said, and rolled along beside him in the car and then he turned and whispered I won't get in with the personification of evil. And my clutch leg started to twitch again and Linn sat in the back and said I should drive, just drive, she said, and I accelerated and saw him staggering along in the rear view mirror with his bow legs.

Norrgården sat there brooding on the top of the hill and I inched the car in behind the earth cellar. Linn disappeared into the old building and Tobias wanted to go to sleep, but I couldn't sleep, and I wandered around on the veranda, back and forth. He would cut across here, at some point he'd come up from the gravel track, and I said to Tobias, sleep? I can't sleep when that bastard is still walking around. He could do anything. And Tobias had some buttermilk and was making up some sandwiches and I stamped about on the veranda, and I don't know what I was waiting for, but it was something, and there was a light on in the old building, a shaft of yellow light in the window furthest away on the gable wall, so Linn must be lying there waiting.

I got some blankets and wrapped them round and sat down on the veranda and was getting sleepy and I must have fallen asleep or something because suddenly it was lighter out there and I opened the veranda door and went out onto the step. It was quiet and the mist was lying on the lake and the meadow and I went down the steps and followed the path across the yard. The door to the artists' veranda was unlocked and open, and I walked into the living room and it smelt like an old barn so they must have kept animals here before, and the smell hadn't gone away, even though it had been a house for a long time now. The planks groaned when I walked over them and when I looked into the kitchen, the beer cans were everywhere on the table and worktop and clothes lay strewn on the kitchen sofa and over the back. The bedroom door was half open, and I pushed it gently and stood there, trying to look into the dark. I heard breathing and saw that she was lying there, Linn, tangled up in a blanket and hair. And there beside her he lay curled up. The blanket had slipped down and his ribs looked pale and grooved. I closed the door and went out onto the barn bridge, where the mist lay in layers over the water and spilled out over the meadow.

My Bruv's Had Enough

AN UNEASINESS AFTER they'd rung, and I wandered around in the flat, and I was supposed to be studying but couldn't study because of the uneasiness that had come over me and wouldn't let go. I sat down with my books and flicked through them and it was really annoying that my bruv was going to come and disturb me. He was always doing that. Fucking annoying, my brother, always running away from hospital. Who the hell does that? Well I mean he does, doesn't he. Of course he's the only one who runs away from the nurses, Bruv, if he's been well for a while and is happy, so now he's got it into his head to run again and the police are after him and rang here to ask if my brother was with me, but he hasn't been here in ages, and if he came I was to call them and let them know and they'd come and get him because there was a warrant out for him now. Evidently my bruv was wanted.

Later in the evening I was standing by the window, staring out, when I saw him. Obviously I recognised him from way off. I know my own brother, after all. He was stamping around out there in the snow and thought he'd make his way over here, although what do I know about what he thought, because he thinks so differently from anyone else, my brother does. I heard the door downstairs slam and footsteps on the stairs. He probably wasn't having much fun at the hospital but they've got one of those ping-pong tables, haven't they. They stand there and play ping-pong. You not playing ping-pong then, Bruv? Yeah, he had the first few months, day-in, day-out, but hadn't hit a ball lately, didn't play ping-pong anymore, right? Bloody shame. I went to visit him a few times, well a couple of times at least, I've been there. Of course I go to visit him, though not very often, in fact pretty damn seldom, but the old man, he'd scarcely been there at all as far as I could work out because he just didn't go, so compared with Dad I'd been there a lot, you could say. He's not even been there once that I've heard of. And now Bruv wasn't there anymore anyway, he was standing outside my door ringing the bell, and I could see him through the peephole, standing there swaying. I opened the door and Bruv peered in.

Anyone else in there, Bruv asked, looking in, and I shook my head and his hospital trousers hung heavy and wet at the bottom so they slid down over his hips and he pulled them up.

Well I was discharged today, right, Bruv said, and grinned and backed away from the door. Oh, you were discharged, I answered. So you sure there's no one else in there then, Bruv said, and hesitated with his big feet in the door. Yes, I'm the only one here, I said, and looked at him, but my brother, his eyes were always looking somewhere else. Police, you've not got any police sitting in there waiting? No, why would I? We can't stand here in the doorway either or the neighbours will start to wonder, won't they, and I don't want them doing that, do I? Whatever. Or you could come out too, couldn't you, my brother said. But I had no intention of going out in that weather and just walking around, because it was as good as midwinter outside and Bruv stood there and shivered and hoisted up his hospital trousers that kept falling down because they were heavy at the hem. So, like, there's no one else in there then, Bruv said, and gave his balls a quick squeeze. You'd better come in anyway if you need to use the loo, I said. Why stand here waiting?

You're not trying to trick me then, Bruv said, and coughed and I shook my head and my brother took a few steps in, then stopped in the doorway and looked into the room. There, behind that door, he said, there's no one there, is there? No, I said. You're not having me on, my brother said. No, why would I do that, I said. You're my sister after all, he said, and when you're family, you should stick together and all that, shouldn't you, back each other up and stick together. Yes, that's right, I said, and my brother took out a pouch of snus from his mouth and squeezed it, then dropped it in his jacket pocket, took out his tin and packed another pouch in.

There, behind that door there, Bruv said. Nope, I said, and I haven't got anyone in the cupboard either, you can be sure of that. And my brother decided that he wanted the old pouch of snus after all, so he took out the new one and left it on the hat shelf and rummaged around in his pocket for the other one.

How's the writing going then, you not sold anything? No, not selling much. How d'you mean, he said. You're not selling anything then, right, he said. Well, I'm selling a bit, I said, but it's not like I've got a big print run to sell. Right, so you're not going to get rich then, Bruv said, stepping back and forth across the threshold.

You've got to come in now, so I can close the door. Okay, Bruv said, and stepped over the threshold in his shoes that were split at the sole. And I don't want any snus on the hat shelf, by the way, I said. No, of course, Bruv said, and hoisted up his trousers. So take it away, I said, and my brother nodded.

Well go on then, in you go, I said, and my brother started and blinked and froze, with his head askew, and blinked. Of course, right, Bruv said, and coughed, right, right. Yes of course, I said, you might as well come in. My brother stepped inside and said right, right, and he stood there and said, right well, my brother said, out in the hall. Hey listen, coffee, you got any coffee, because I'd like one then, a coffee, he said, and grinned when it was obvious that I had coffee.

So you were discharged today then, I said, and my brother froze and stood there, blinking, with his head tilted. Yeah, I'm better now, you know, Bruv said. It's just the medicine, the pills, they make you kind of restless, they're new, see, I've changed medication. You'll take away that snus, won't you? I said. Right, Bruv said, and turned round and picked up the snus with his fingers and felt it because he might still want it, no matter how bad it looked, and took out the other snus he had in his mouth, and stepped through the door into the kitchen, looked around, put the snus down on the draining board, and then popped the old pouch in.

So you like them when they're kind of cold and soggy, then, I said, and my brother grinned and sucked on the snus and he was actually looking good, my brother, he always did, but he didn't smell so good. Ugh, you smell fucking disgusting, Bruv. You got to wash yourself, you hear. You smell disgusting. Think you're going to get any girls when you smell like that? Uh-uh, not a single one, I said. Really, you don't think so, my brother asked. No. Girls don't like it, see, when you smell like that. You'll have to go and wash yourself, I said. Really, so you don't think I'll get any girls, my brother said. No bloody way will you get any girls, I said. Not when you smell like that. No, you don't get any girls then, Bruv said, and grinned because he always used to get the girls, my brother did, before anyway, but he won't get them now, not when you smell like that, I said, and Bruv turned on the kitchen tap and ran some water through his hair. He had curly hair, which he stroked and patted and primped.

Hmm, my brother said, and turned and looked me straight in the eye, which he didn't very often do, but suddenly he looked me right in the eye and grinned. What is it, I asked, and Bruv screwed up his eyes and said, they're nice those jeans you've got on, but you always wear nice things, he said, and he'd taken his shoes off in the hall so his feet left moist prints on the floor. Why don't you put your socks on the radiator, I said, and put on some coffee and Bruv's trousers hung wet and dirty and he hoisted them up. And he wanted to go out onto the balcony for a smoke, my brother, so I went out into the sitting room and opened the door for him and watched him stand out there and shiver and take a drag, and I should phone, it would be best if I just phoned, and told them so they knew where he was, because he'd been reported missing, my brother. But Bruv came back in again almost straight away and had smoked it down in one, as it were, and was cold.

So you know that I'm going to start my own business, right, Bruv said, and left the stub of his cigarette by the sink and I nodded and looked out of the window. Well, don't suppose you've got anything to eat, hmm, Bruv asked, and cleared his throat. Because I've not eaten since this morning, right, and I'm starting to get really hungry now, Bruv said. So if I had anything at all, he wasn't fussy, my brother, never had been. I set about frying some fish fingers for him and defrosting some of that pea and sweet corn mix and my brother walked back and forth between the hall and the kitchen, back out into the hall and then into the kitchen again, pulling up his trousers.

Right, Bruv said, and took the snus out from under his lip and squeezed the pouch that he'd put on the sink and rummaged around in his pocket for another fix, because he switched between a few pouches for variety, see. So, you don't think they'll come here then, because they'll manage to find it, won't they, Bruv said, and I wondered who he meant. So the nurses from the ward aren't here then, Bruv said, and whispered, because I thought I saw them out there when I was having a smoke. I thought I saw them.

No, they don't have the time, do they, to come and snoop around here. You think they've got time for that, I said. But they want you to stay there forever, don't they. They want you locked up, you know, and that's the truth, Bruv said. And I said that they were sure to let you out

when you were well again, because they don't want people
sitting around and costing money, I said, but Bruv just stood
there rocking gently in the kitchen trying to decide which
pouch of snus he wanted, because he had three on the go,
lying there on the worktop, slimy and cold, and a cigarette
butt beside them. Because Bruv knew someone who had
been there for eight years, right, and she was totally okay,
he said. She might well be okay, I thought, but maybe she's
not that fucking okay, not if she's there, I said. How was I
to know?

So they haven't been here then, the nurses, Bruv said,
and he coughed and I laughed and Bruv grinned and put his
hand between his legs. No, so you can give over then, I said,
and Bruv grinned and lifted his gaze, which was normally
fixed to the ground. Because Bruv said he thought there
was someone sneaking around in the sitting room, and he
pulled at the elasticated waist of his trousers, or maybe they
were pyjama bottoms he was wearing, and everywhere he
put his hands got dirty, and there were marks on the floor,
and I don't know where you've been or what you've done,
Bruv, but you're fucking filthy and you better go and wash
yourself, now, I said, and made to throw away the snus,
because I didn't want the pouches lying around by the sink.
But Bruv got there first and was stubborn, and grabbed hold
of my hand because he wanted to be able to choose. I like
mixing and matching, otherwise it gets boring. You get
bored otherwise, right, Bruv said, and sat down.

I piled the food on a plate for him and sat down at
the opposite side of the table. Bruv put the snus down on
the table and leant forward over the plate and ate while I
looked out of the window. Is anyone coming, Bruv asked,
bent over the plate, eating, and I grinned at him. You're
bloody disgusting when you eat, Bruv, I said, and he looked
straight up at me, narrowing his eyes. Yeah, you know what,
I cultivate the animal in me, see, he said, and I grinned at
my brother because he could always defend himself. He was

good with words and things like that. And I sat and watched my brother as he ate, one hand scraping the table-top. He liked eating, Bruv, always had, and he grunted and chewed and ate and I watched the snow falling outside the window.

You see, Bruv said, the nurses, they're after me now, and I think they know where you live. They haven't rung have they, Bruv said, and I shook my head. You're not kidding me now? No, why would I do that, I said. Bruv said that he thought you should stick together when you were family, stick together and support each other and all that, Bruv said, and I nodded. Hmm, Bruv said, and suddenly looked straight at me with those strange bright eyes that he'd got from somewhere. D'you remember that time we were in Greece and had rented that apartment together? Man the parties we had, Bruv said, and I nodded.

We had great drinking fests and all that, in that flat, didn't we, Bruv said, and I nodded and looked out the window. Can you see anyone, Bruv said, and I shook my head and asked if he wanted some coffee. Yeah, whatever, coffee or tea, but tea if you got it, I'd prefer tea, Bruv said, and got up and walked back and forth between the hall and the kitchen, then peered into the other room. Are you not going to sit down and finish your food then, I said. Of course, Bruv said, and carried on walking backwards and forwards. So it's tea you want then, I said. That'd be good, Bruv said, and went out onto the balcony. I stood by the phone and watched him take a few deep drags and then he came in again, smelling of cigarettes.

You know what, if you've got coffee after all, Bruv said, and knew that I did, and I told him I'd just made the tea, and Bruv said, right I see, it's fine with tea then. Are you going to sit down again, Bruv, or are you going to keep walking backwards and forwards? But if you've got coffee, Bruv said, and sat down and started eating again.

So you don't want tea then, I said, and Bruv stopped and blinked and said that yes, that's fine, sure, and blinked.

Yeah, I'll have tea instead, after all, you hear that, I'll have tea, Bruv said, and I looked out of the window at some cars that had driven into the parking place. And it was silent. My brother lifted his head from the plate in silence. I've run away from there, you see, he said, and grinned. You escaped, I said. I ran away from them when we were out for a walk. I jumped over some bushes and legged it, Bruv said, and I wondered whether they'd run after him and Bruv said they did, but he was quick, see, and then there were the bushes, because I tricked them when I jumped over the bushes, because they couldn't see where I'd gone, Bruv said, and I wondered whether it was a smart thing to do, to run away, but Bruv, he thought that it was the only way to get away from there, because otherwise they'd keep you locked up there forever, just sitting there, Bruv said, because they want to hurt you, see, the staff, they don't treat you well, Bruv said, they humiliate you. Of course some of them might get a bit fraught from working there all the time, but they don't mean to hurt you, I said, I don't believe that.

Yes they do, they humiliate you and like it and they take away your fags, right, Bruv said, and decided that he was going to have another smoke. So he started rummaging around in his pockets for butts and stubs and went out to light up and I saw him stand out there on the balcony, my brother, with his broad shoulders and neck, his sweater hanging off him, and he was stooped and he wasn't like that before, you weren't allowed to stoop at home, because if you were caught stooping you'd get Dad's finger in your back. My brother stood rocking on the balcony, keeping an eye out, and he turned and squinted at me.

Right, well, Bruv said, when he came back in and sat down at his plate and started to eat again. And I watched him chew and scrape the plate until he was finished, going after the peas and chasing them round and round the plate, because they were here, there, everywhere, green, and Bruv's fork shook as he chased them and then speared one and put it in his mouth and chewed and then hunted down the next one and had trouble with his coordination and catching them, and the fork slid and slipped over the peas.

You must be done now, I said to him, and pulled the plate over, but Bruv, he pulled it back because he wasn't done, see. He hunched over the plate and hunted down the peas and slid the fork between them. Because there were still peas left and he wanted to eat them. Because he loved food, my brother, and when he was little he always took huge portions and shovelled up the whole lot. Because he loved food, and when we sat at the big wooden table at Dad's farm and I sat and watched my brother, sometimes I looked at my dad, and Bruv, he sat there with his messy thick hair hanging down over the plate and he ate and smiled and chewed and licked and looked up every now and then. Because when my brother sat like that in front of a mountain of food, he was happy, and the food steamed up his face and he smelt and tasted it. And he tasted and mashed his food and turned and grinned at me over his food, because my brother loved his food and I looked over at him and I looked over at Dad, and Bruv ate and chewed with his eyes closed and swallowed. And then eventually my brother had had enough. I sat and saw that my brother was full and Dad, he could see it too. My brother picked at the food a bit and licked his fork and thumb, and he rubbed his nose and wiped away the snot, and lifted his eyes and looked out of the window. The food that was left on the plate was congealed and lukewarm and Bruv looked away. And Dad, he leant back in his chair and looked at Bruv, and it didn't stop there.

Yes, you have to eat everything, Bruv said, sitting in my kitchen, and he lifted his head and grinned and I grinned back. He's not easy to argue with, Dad, he's not very good at it, Bruv said. In fact, he's not very good at talking at all. Nope, I actually think he wants to hurt us, don't you? Has he called, or anything? I shook my head and said that Dad didn't mean to harm anyone, that he wanted the best for people, only the best, Dad, you know that, I said.

So he's not on his way here then, Bruv said, and I shook my head. Bruv managed to catch the last pea with his fork and I took away the plate that was greasy and empty and he followed it with his eyes. So anyway, but they've got dead bodies in the ward, he said, because I saw a hand sticking out. Of course they don't, I said, you know that. What are you talking about, I said. Stop saying things like that. You're not in a mortuary, are you? Bruv grinned and slurped his coffee and then a bit later slurped some tea.

Yeah, but I think as family, we've got to stick together more, Bruv said, and took the snus tin out of his jacket pocket, because he'd started to use snus when cigarettes weren't enough, and no matter how much he smoked it wasn't enough, so Bruv used snus as well, even though that wasn't enough either.

Can I stay here tonight, Bruv asked. I can stay here, can't I, just for a few nights. But I'm studying, I said, and where do you think you'd sleep? It's only a studio flat, after all, I said, but Bruv reckoned he could sleep in the kitchen. You can't just sleep in the kitchen, because I have to get up early and we've got different routines and all that, and you know that I get up early and you don't, you never have, I said. And then the phone rang and my brother jumped and blinked and I picked up the receiver and I heard that it was Dad on the other end. So he'd obviously pulled himself together, Dad, and phoned and was sitting with the receiver in his hand trying to say something, and Bruv, he looked over at me and listened and Dad wondered on the other end of the line whether I'd seen my brother. Yes, I said into the receiver, and Bruv stood there listening and scratched his balls. He's run away, you see, Dad said, is he there? Yes, that's fine, I said into the receiver, and Dad asked if I could keep him there so he could call the police. Yes, do that, I said. Aha, I see, Dad said, he's standing there listening. Yep, I said to Dad, and Bruv stood in the doorway and hoisted up his trousers. I'll phone straightaway, so they'll be there soon. Yes, thanks, I said, and put down the receiver and Bruv stood with his head askance, blinking.

Well, so, who were you talking to then, Bruv asked, and I looked at him in the doorway, and the damp brown prints left behind where he'd walked over the parquet. He always left something behind him. Footprints and crumbs and dirt.

It was the neighbour, I said. The neighbour over the way, and I pointed, and Bruv blinked and asked what they were called, and who was it? The neighbour across the landing, I said, and Bruv grinned and his eyes crinkled and shone. Are you trying to trick me, Bruv said, and grinned. No, and I don't want any snus on my desk, I said, as he'd left some lying there, shiny, you hear, and I don't want any snus by the sink either, right? There was one by the soap that was oozing and brown. And he still had coffee and tea left. Are you not going to drink it, I asked, as Bruv stood in the doorway like he'd been glued there.

Right, well, I can trust you, can't I, Bruv said, and blinked. Of course you can, I said, and looked out of the window and Bruv tottered across the floor like an old man, though he's not old, he just turned thirty this year. Shall we go out for a walk, he asked, and I shook my head. Come on, Bruv said, let's go out for a walk, and then later I can go to Stefan's because I'll be able to stay there. But you can go out later, can't you, I said. I mean, it's cold and snowing, and Bruv picked up a book that was lying on the desk and opened it. Oh, so you're studying at the moment, then, Bruv said. As usual, studying at the moment. Hmm, says lots of things here, Bruv said. But are you writing anything, Bruv asked, and I nodded. You're not writing about me, are you, Bruv said, and grinned. No, I said, as he hadn't read anything yet, my brother.

You know what, I'm writing at the moment too, Bruv said, but you don't sell anything, do you? No, I don't sell much, but I have sold a few thousand. Right. I'm actually writing a novel, I am, Bruv said. You can read it if you like. Thanks, I said. But my novel's going to sell, right, Bruv said, and hoisted his hospital trousers. You can read it if you want, y'know. Right, thanks, I said, and Bruv sat down in front of the mugs and tried to choose between them. My novel's going to sell, right. I mean, yours don't. No, I said, and looked out of the window and Bruv rummaged around in his pocket for some snus.

Nah, they don't want your best on the ward, Bruv said. They don't treat you well at all. They humiliate you. Do they, I said. And I saw a body in one of the rooms there, once. When I sneaked into the office, there was a patient lying there, and it was a body, right. You know they don't have dead bodies there. You're making it up again, I said, and Bruv grinned and tobacco juice dribbled down over his teeth and out the corner of his mouth. Right, Bruv said, and grinned. If you think logically, yeah, they don't have dead bodies there, do they, I said and Bruv took out the snus and squeezed it.

Maybe, but once they did, Bruv said. Sometimes they do. I saw it. My brother lifts the mug of coffee and then the mug of tea because he has to choose to drink one of them, after all. The hand was hanging down like this, Bruv said, and showed me, and I reached over and got hold of Bruv's snus tin and asked if I could have one, not that I used snus anymore, but the taste for snus was always there, whether you use it or not, I reckoned, and it was Bruv who had got me using it in the first place and it had burned, and then later it had been so damn hard to learn to not use it again.

I mean, do you sell anything, Bruv said. You've already asked that, I said. Right, Bruv grinned, a sensitive subject then, is it? No, it's not, I said. Yeah it is. That sort of thing can be sensitive, Bruv said, and got up and walked back and forth between the kitchen and the hall. Well, I don't care whether you think it's sensitive or not, I said.

The door downstairs, it's locked, isn't it, Bruv said, as he struggled into his shoes out in the hall, and walked in them over to the window, and pulled the curtains shut. And I said always, and I opened them again.

Don't come in here with your shoes on, I said. No course not, Bruv said, and blinked. I don't want you walking around in here with your shoes on, you hear, I said, and my brother just stood there blinking. Right, whatever, Bruv said. I'll go over to Stefan's now. Because I think the nurses know that I'm here. I saw them from the balcony sneaking around down there in garden. But you can't go, I said. Yeah, think I'll be on my way, like, I mean, you don't think they'll come here, right? I don't want snus lying on the radiator, I said. Have you left some snus on the radiator because I don't want any on the radiator, either, I said, and saw it lying there drying. And Bruv pulled on his jacket and stood there and dithered and rocked and sucked on his snus. You might as well stay here, right, now that you've come, I said, and Bruv stood out in the hall blinking. It's nice that you're here, I mean, to have you here so long, I said, and Bruv froze and stopped. You think so, Bruv said, and blinked.

Course I do, I said, and Bruv stood with his head cocked and blinked. Well well, Bruv said, well well, he said. Yeah, I said. I mean, I think I should go anyway, Bruv said. Are you going, I said. You're not going to go, I mean, where are you going to go, d'you think? To Stefan's maybe, I thought, I mean he's bound to be home. He works, doesn't he, I said. Nah, Stefan doesn't work, right, he's on what they call sick leave. Anyway, I'll go and see if Stefan's at home, because Stefan's got all my records so I can go to Stefan and listen to my records. Stefan might have some wine as well, he usually does, and he'll give me a glass. We usually sit there and drink wine, see, listening to records. You do, do you, I said, and Bruv grinned. Then later, well, we might go down to The Gravediggers, maybe we'll do that, Bruv said. There's girls there at The Gravediggers who you can talk to. I mean we normally talk to the girls, he grinned, and hoisted up his hospital trousers and I looked out of the window and saw a car turn into the parking place, and it swung round and stopped outside the door, its headlights sweeping the snow.

We're Moving on Tomorrow

IT WAS SUMMER and the holidays and Dad stood out by the Volvo loading stuff up, and me and my little sisters carried out bags and boxes and put them down on the pavement. I didn't want to go with the family, really. I wanted to spend those weeks at home, on my own, instead, and cycle down for a swim with Elin and lie there on the jetty and drink beer and sunbathe, but I couldn't. Because now Dad was packing our blue Volvo estate and I carried things down and helped him to fix the canoe to the roof-rack and my little sisters were running around with fishing rods and things and getting the lines tangled.

I sat there in the back of the Volvo, squashed between my little sisters, and they sat there being cheeky and horrible and reading their pony magazines. The Volvo drove through Sweden and the sun shone in through the windows and my little sisters whinged and smelt of sweaty kids.

And it was evening by the time we got to the campsite where we were going to spend a few nights, and Dad drove in through the gate, and there was a forest lake that glittered and shone pink in the sun. My little sisters were asleep in the back of the car and sucking their thumbs and everyone had those big house tents, but not us. We had those small green mountain tents with a porch, didn't we, that hugged the ground and the midges came straight away and started to dance while we put them up. Now, let's try and get on with the neighbours, Mum said. Well I haven't said anything, Dad said. He carried my little sisters into one of the tents and they woke up and started whimpering.

I lay in the tent between my little sisters and they couldn't get back to sleep but wanted to go for a pee the whole time and pulled down the zip on the tent and rustled and tripped and let in the midges. They didn't dare go too far in the dark, but sat just behind the tent, they did, and I lay there and heard the grass gurgle.

When they fell asleep I slipped down to the water and sat there on some rocks. The water was still and black and I had some cigarettes and pretended to smoke. I lit one and blew the smoke out into the night and the summer wrapped its warmth around me and the dragonflies danced on the water. And I sat there and blew smoke at the midges, and I hadn't noticed that there was anyone else down by the water but someone was walking down there, and it could be anyone, could be Dad. I stubbed out the fag and pulled up the hood on my sweatshirt. But it wasn't Dad. Instead it was some girl in a red sweater who came slipping over the rocks. I lit the fag again, because it was good just to hold it I thought. It looked like she'd been for a swim, with her towel hanging over her shoulder, and she came closer and I saw her and she saw me and I thought I should say something but I didn't know what. So I sat there and tried to find some words that I could casually drop. Was it cold, I managed to squeeze out, and she shook her head. You sitting here on your own, she said. Why are you sitting here? Well I didn't really know why I was sitting there, but you have to sit somewhere, I said, and I didn't want to sit squashed up with my little sisters in the tent. She kept her head turned away the whole time, her hair hung black and soft down her back, and she spoke with some kind of an accent that scraped in her mouth. Could you spare a fag, she said, and of course I could if she wanted one. I handed her a ciggie and tried to see what she looked like, because it was like I wasn't allowed to see, because she kept turned away and her hair hung down over her face and was dripping. Do you want to come up to the caravan and play cards with my brothers, she said, and of course I'd tag along if that was okay.

She walked in front of me up the path towards the camping site and the caravan and I'd spotted the caravan before. It was a big wooden caravan, probably home-made Dad had said. It was standing right at the edge, and on the steps was a cage with two white desert rats. She bent down and opened the door and stuck a finger in and stroked them on the back, and I saw her face then in the light from the lamppost, one side of her face kind of twisted, and her eye was droopy and running and the skin was all bumpy and scarred and her ear was an ornate gash in her head. She pushed open the door and turned the other side of her face to me and it was just like it should be with her brown shiny eye below her black fringe, and lips that slipped softly over her teeth. Have you met my brothers, she said, and obviously I hadn't met her brothers but it must be them sitting there on cushions on the floor, smoking and playing cards. And there were daybeds along the sides, and in the middle was a stove, and one of the brothers was playing the guitar and grinned at me and sang in a language that I couldn't make out. She sat down beside me on the cushions on the floor and her eye was running the whole time, and she had a hanky and wiped it, and she poured some wine into two glasses because the brothers obviously had some wine that they were drinking, and she handed me one of the glasses, and I'd never really drunk wine before but now I was sitting there and drinking wine that was warm and red, and she wiped her eye and leant over to me, and she smelt of fresh water and shampoo. He's my youngest brother, she said, and pointed, and the brother sang and she drank her red wine and poured some more. Her hair hung in front of half her face but I knew that it was scarred and festering and the mouth was twisted and loose, so I looked at the other side because the skin was smooth and brown there, and the cheek was flushed. She laughed and topped up my glass and said you're not used to drinking wine, are you, she said, and I shook my head and took a sip, and have you got a boyfriend, have you, she asked, and leant forwards and I shook my head and her eye was running and she wiped it with the hanky and drank and looked at me. But you've had one, haven't you, she said, and I grinned because of course I had, but no one that would really count right now, I said. And she poured some more wine and took a sip and her hair had dried and hung heavy and dark around her. But don't you think you'll get one again sometime, she said. And I said yes, of course, sometime. She nodded and turned her glass and was silent. And then suddenly she looked straight up at me with her good eye. Why haven't you asked about my face, she said, and I stared at her. You're sitting there wondering, aren't you, wondering and thinking. Of course I'm wondering, I said. But you haven't asked because you don't dare, she said, and moved closer, and I could feel her spit on my cheek and the wine swilled around inside me, or maybe it was the caravan that rocked and her spit on my cheek. She reached over and poured some more wine and took a drink and said you're just like all the others, she said. Yeah, I guess I'm like all the others, I said. You just look and wonder and think, she said, don't you, think that she'll never get a boyfriend, don't you, did you think that, that she'll never find anyone, she said, and drank some more wine and turned the glass. I've never had one, you know, and never will, she said, and the wine swilled around inside, warm and red. And I looked at her and said that I hadn't thought that at all, I said, because of course you'll find someone, of course you will, I said, and her brothers sat there with their cards and played the guitar and smoked. She held her hair back from her face and took my hand and lifted it up to her ear and stroked my fingers over the deformed circles of her ear and her ear against my fingertips was warm and soft. Then she dropped my hand and laughed and said you're still not used to drinking wine, she said, and I grinned and shook my head. She got up and took hold of me and I staggered out onto the caravan steps and the summer night outside was pale and warm and the desert rats sat huddled in their shavings. She sat down on the steps and I sat down beside her, and she opened the cage and took out the rats and put them on her knee and stroked their white backs. I was born like this, she said. They've operated five times and they're going to operate on my ear again for my hearing because I can't hardly hear anything with it. I nodded and reached out and stroked the rats that were on her knees, and they smelled, and tickled my fingers with their whiskers. We're moving on tomorrow, she said. So are we, I said.

She stayed on the steps as I walked away between the caravans and tents, and I turned round and waved and she wiped her eye and waved back.

In the morning I was woken by the canvas clinging damp to my face. My little sisters were lying there and reading their pony magazines and the sun was shimmering on the outer tent. I heard Dad's voice outside. Don't tell me you forgot the bag, he said, and Mum said I haven't forgotten anything. It's not possible to forget a whole bag, Dad said, and Mum said I can't look after everyone's bags and things the whole time. A whole bloody bag, Dad said. It was you who packed the car, Mum said, and my little sisters sighed and turned the pages of their pony magazines even though they couldn't really read. I look after everyone's things all the time and I don't want to anymore, you know, your things and the children's, a whole lot of bloody stuff, Mum said outside.

And later me and my little sisters sat round the Trangia stove and drank hot chocolate and ate cheese sandwiches and my Dad sat on his folding chair and said that Mum had forgotten a whole bag with raingear and stuff, Dad said, and leant back on his folding chair and Mum drank her coffee and said I haven't forgotten anything. And the neighbours had a fancy tent with curtains and geraniums in pots and they were sitting there in their porch looking out at the summer through plastic windows. Sitting there behind the plastic, breeding, Dad said, and stared at the neighbours.

Afterwards I lay down by the water and sunbathed and it smelled rotten from the rubbish bins, with the wasps buzzing drowsily around them. The jetty creaked and complained when children ran out on it, and the beach was packed with people and children and cool bags. My little sisters were playing in the water with their inflatable crocodiles, and toddlers sat in the warm shallows with their pink sun hats on, and stared and peed.

Where are you going, my little sisters shouted after me, when I ran up the path, past the toilets and over towards the edge of the woods. I could see from way off that it wasn't there anymore, just some deep tyre tracks in the grass. The guy in the next caravan was busy fastening his awning. Have they gone, I said, and he nodded, and look what they've done to the grass.

Dad was packing the car again and my little sisters pulled at me and wanted to go to the clearing and they weren't allowed to go there on their own so I ended up walking with them into the forest to keep an eye on my little sisters. The sun dappled the clearing and the pines stood and whispered their loneliness and I saw that there had been elks there. My little sisters were slow, and behind all the time, and they stumbled and tripped on the undergrowth and I stood and waited and shouted and kicked a rotten tree stump, sending the ants running frantically everywhere. And I didn't want to look after my little sisters all day. Come and get some chocolate, I shouted, because my little sisters liked chocolate, and I heard them fighting their way through undergrowth that snagged and hit them in the face. I wasn't really the sort who normally offered chocolate, but here I was, shouting come and get some chocolate, because they knew I was a master at saving and collecting and then taking things out of my pocket to chew. And my little sisters came scrambling over the clearing towards me, and I stood there and held out big chocolate balls and my little sisters stared at them because it was obvious that they looked a bit weird, but they've been lying in my pocket for a while, I said, and my little sisters nodded and looked at the chocolate that was lying there, shiny in my hand. Don't you want any chocolates then, I said. And of course they did, and they reached out and took one each and bit into it and chewed, and I saw them turning the chocolate round in their mouths, and it looked a bit dry and fibrous and I grinned and my little sisters stared at me and twisted their mouths and chewed. And then they spat it out because it doesn't taste like chocolate, my little sisters said, and I grinned and said no, maybe it tastes like elk shit. I bolted back to the campsite and the car was standing ready and packed and my little sisters ran after me, stumbling, spitting and running.

The Roslag Bus

SHE HAD NEVER gone to her cousins' on her own before but now she was going there, walking along in her white trainers and new skirt to the bus station and looking for the bus. Her ponytail was hanging and tickling her pale neck because they hadn't got any sun yet here in the town, but out at her cousins' her neck would get sun and saltwater, if only she got on the right bus, because there were buses standing everywhere, ready to go all over the place, and she wandered between them and looked for the right number. The sun hung high and shone down on the buses and on her as she walked, and her mint-green skirt swung and fanned her legs. Beside the bus with the right number there was a long queue that snaked round and she went to the end of the queue and stood there and the sun shone down and it was warm and she stood there in the queue in her new skirt, looking down at it every now and then, and in her hand she had a bag with her overnight stuff and swimming costume and a book that she wrote things down in. The driver opened the door and the people barged and pushed their way onto the bus with their bags and baskets and she was small and quick and snuck in and got a window seat. The bus filled up and there she sat in her window seat and she put her bag on the overhead shelf and took off her cardigan and sat there in only a vest top because it was hot on the bus and close, and more people kept getting on and squeezed in and stood in the aisle. They were going to come and meet her, her aunt and some of her cousins, and they'd see her skirt and be impressed that she had such a lovely skirt on out there in the country, because she was from the town after all. And the bus started and pulled out on its way and it was hot and smelled of diesel and people were standing in the aisle and lost their balance and got squashed whenever the bus braked and she moved even closer to the window and sat looking out at the town, and the bus pulled out onto the motorway and the sun burned through the windows and the asphalt lay black and soft, and she watched it rush past and leant forwards and put her hands on her new skirt and brushed it down because now she was on her way. The bus lurched and people stood and swayed and the dust was suspended, glittering in the sun, and she was going a long way and she liked travelling and sitting and just travelling, but it was so packed and squashed the whole time that she moved in towards the window and looked out at the forests and fields and the summer, and there was a nudge and a little stroke and she moved her arm and the bus lurched and she turned and looked at the man sitting next to her, but he was asleep. She smoothed her new skirt and looked out of the window because out there somewhere was the summer and her cousins and they would surely go down and swim later and lie on the jetty and talk and eat plums, and her cousins had cats and sheep and all sorts, they had, on their land, old Volvo Amazons that stood there with moss on the seats and in the evening they would sit by her cousins' big table and eat her aunt's bread and drink lemon balm tea and then she and her cousins would go out to the three-seater loo in the outhouse and there they'd each sit on their own seat next to each other and feel the breeze on their bums and smell the peat. But right now she was sitting there on the bus and the sweat was dripping under her ponytail and there was a stroke again and a nudge and someone was fingering her and she moved in to the window and the fingers followed and she got her cardigan and wrapped it round her but the fingers came searching through the cardigan and in underneath it and the bus turned off and rattled along the narrow roads and the fingers followed and no matter how she twisted and turned they were there, at her side, and she tried to put her arm in the way but still they kept coming and feeling and climbing up her side and on her breasts and she turned and looked at him, sitting beside her, and he was asleep and slumped forwards with his arms folded and she wasn't being touched right now when she looked at him. She looked out through the window at the summer and her cousins were going to come and meet her, and soon she would get off and get away from the fingers and the sweat on the back of her knees and the sun and the dust that glittered in it, because there was the big white house and the hill and now she had to get off. She stretched over and pressed the stop button. And maybe there hadn't been any fingers because she couldn't feel them now, nor when she twisted on her cardigan and got hold of her bag from above, and the man beside her was asleep and slumped forwards, his eyes closed, and she clambered past him and of course there hadn't been any fingers or anything, it had just been the sweat that tickled the back of her knees, and she stood by the door and waited and the bus pulled in and stopped and she went down the steps and the doors opened, and her legs were shaking when she stepped out of the bus and into the summer, and the crickets were singing in the ditch. She stood on the hot dirt and turned around and looked up through the bus window and there was the man she had sat beside and he was awake now and leaning towards the window looking out at her and grinning. She stood there in her white trainers on the dirt track and the bus accelerated and drove off and her mint-green skirt fluttered around her legs.

You and Me

DAVID SAT THERE in the kitchen opposite her and outside the flat was the city and all the sounds of the city and the neighbour playing the piano. David looked at her and she looked back and she thought about Johan's hands. He had such different hands, big and broad, not like David's slim fingers and David wondered what she was thinking about. About you, she said, your hands, that's what I was thinking about, she said, and he nodded. You and your hands, she said. And Johan's big hands, they had held her, well, properly. They had held her and he was much older than her, Johan, eighteen years older, and they were just friends him and her, and I need that, she said, to meet older friends, well, because she didn't have anything else. Yes, David said, of course you're friends, and of course you should meet if you're friends. And he's that much older, David said, and she nodded. And you need to meet someone that old, David said. Yes, she said, I've got no older friends apart from Johan. You seem to need it, he said, and she nodded, and I need you, she said, and the neighbour had stopped playing, so it must be nine o'clock, she said, and he nodded. The neighbour was a cantor and played in the evenings until nine o'clock and they sat there drinking tea every evening, they sat there, him by the window and her opposite, had lived there for several years now and sat there in the evening drinking tea and eating biscuits, and she looked at him every evening as they sat there and she never got tired of looking at him because he always looked different, small things in his face were different. She looked at him and he asked what she was looking at. You're looking at me like I'm an object, he

85

said. I like looking at you, she said, and she was tired of those biscuits, let's buy some other ones now. Yes, buy some other ones, why don't you, he said, and she nodded. And outside you could hear the sounds of the city, and the bar down below had just opened so the doormen were standing outside chatting to each other and laughing. You talk so much about Johan, he said, and she nodded and said that she had to meet Johan because she needed him and that was obvious, he said, and I haven't said anything about it, have I? And he hadn't, after all, but it just felt like he didn't like it, so sometimes she said she was going to meet someone else, and then she felt a bit uneasy the whole time because she'd lied and didn't feel comfortable with it. And Johan and her normally went to the park when they met, and talked because they were just friends, but they still touched all the time, touched hands and clothes, and Johan often asked her up to his for tea, said that she should come up to his flat, and she had, she had gone with him and sat there drinking tea and the last time she sat there Johan had looked at her and she looked down at the table and he was older than her so he had some weight, sat there with his weight and she sat beside him and was light, and they sat there in silence and looked at each other and just looked and Johan's hand stroked her and his fingers crept in under the sleeves and his skin was completely different from David's. His skin was loose and dark, and she stroked over it and didn't really know how she should stroke skin that was so different but she stroked it all the same and he looked at her and trembled under her touch.

No, I haven't said anything, have I, David said, sitting at the table. At least I didn't mean to, and of course you should meet this Johan guy, you obviously like talking to him, he said, and she nodded and sipped her tea. What do you talk about all the time then, you and Johan, he said, and she said that they talked about lots of things, all sorts of things, because he was easy to talk to, she said, and David nodded. Because he does all sorts of things, he does stuff with films and things like that, she said, and he nodded. What does he actually do, does he make films or what, David said. And she said that she didn't really know, but it was something to do with film, she said, and he nodded. He can come here sometimes, David said, what do you think? He can come here, he said, and she nodded and looked at her hands that were dry now in winter, always dry, and with small cracks on the back of her hands that stung. Because it's interesting that he's into film, David said, and she nodded and she had to ask him more about the film because she'd not done that. She didn't actually say much to him, the last time she was there, but mostly just sat on the sofa and he had stroked her and touched her all over, he had touched her and she had sat still because he didn't touch like David, he touched in a completely different way and she needed that way too. And she had run home late in the snow and when she got home David was sitting at his desk and she had hugged him and she knew David all over, his hands and fair skin, and she liked to brush against him. And she usually talked to him about everything she wanted to tell him. To share, and hear what he thought.

You talk so much about this Johan, David said, sitting at the table, and she looked at him. Well it doesn't really matter, it just struck me. But he's just what you need, he said. Yes, she said. Then there's something that I don't have, that you need, David said. But he's much older, she said. Yes it's because he's older, he said. Yes, she said. Or is it something else, he said, something that I don't have and you need. It's probably because he's so old, she said. Yes, he said, or else there's something else that you need because you need so much. Do I, she said. Yes, you always just need something. He got up and walked around in the kitchen. No, I don't, she said. Why are you saying that? Oh, I don't know, he said, it must be because he's older. Yes, she said, and there was silence in the kitchen as the neighbour had stopped playing the piano but the doormen down below by the bar, they were standing talking and freezing, and their voices bounced off the walls and every now and then a car horn hooted. Where did you actually meet this Johan then, David said, and she was sure that she'd told him before, several times before, at the party, you knew that, she said, and he shook his head. We just happened to sit down next to each other, she said. We just sat there and talked at the party, she said, and he nodded. But they hadn't really been able to speak, had hardly spoken, and he just looked at her and she looked back and she had drunk loads of red wine and he had poured her more and sat there and looked at her and there was something about his teeth, as if there was something behind them. We can't really talk at all, he had said, and searched, and she had looked at his teeth and nodded. And yet you're the only one I want to talk to at this party, he said, and she nodded. I don't want to talk to anyone else but you, he said, and laughed and she smiled and he took her hand and stroked her palm with his thumb and she sat still and felt his warm thumb stroking her palm.

Now when you talk about this Johan, something happens to your mouth, David said, sitting at the table. I've thought about it and seen that something always happens to your mouth. I don't know, she said, does something happen to my mouth? Yes, it's something with your mouth, he said. Why are you looking at my mouth? It looks different all the time. Yes, but when you talk about this Johan there's something sort of tight about your mouth. Well, what do you want me to say, she said. It doesn't really matter, he said, I just noticed, that's all. I should start looking at your mouth a bit more as well, she said. You look at me all the time, he said, and the doormen laughed outside and chatted away because there wasn't much of a queue for the bar, and she leant out and saw that there were some people in the queue down below and they were cold and waiting and the doormen were chatting to them.

You'll get tired of looking at me soon enough, he said. No, what makes you say that, she said. Well, I don't know, he said. I'm not tired of looking at you, she said. No, but you will be soon, he said. It doesn't feel like that at all, she said. No, but that's what will happen, he said. I don't believe it will ever, she said. Believe, he said. Yeah, he said. But you can't know for certain. No, obviously, he said, that's just the way it is. But no one can know that, she said. No, I know, he said, and drank some tea and she looked out of the window. They lived three floors up so it was a long way down to where they were standing in the queue grumbling and freezing. You came back late from that party, he said. Yes, it was a fun party, she said. So it was a good party, he said, and she nodded. And she had run for the night bus home after the party, and David had gone to bed and was asleep when she got in, and she had snuggled up to him and she knew him all over, she knew him and how he smelt and felt.

What was it that was so good about that party, then, he said, but she couldn't remember anymore, just that it was good, she said. It must've been that Johan that was so good then, he said. Yeah, maybe it was, she said, but I have to be able to go to parties and have some fun now and then. Yes, of course, he said, you so rarely go to parties, and I want you to have fun, he said, and she nodded. And there was silence, but for the doormen standing down below. Talking, joking voices that echoed on the walls. Yes, you always just need something, he said, and she said that she didn't. Why do you say that, she said. Oh, I don't know, he said, but you said you're going to meet this Johan again tomorrow. Did I say that, she said. You know whether you've arranged something or not. Yes, she said. It's been a while since you met up with Angelika, he said. But I've got so much to do right now, she said. I haven't got time to see her all the time, have I? No, of course, he said. That's just the way it is, she said. But tomorrow, he said, you're going to meet Johan. Yes, she said. I don't know. No, I don't know either, he said, but now you need to meet Johan. Yes, she said, and nodded and tomorrow she would go to his place again and sit on his sofa like the last time, when she sat in his sofa and listened to music and his hands crept all over her and touched her over her knickers, under her dress, his hands that slipped around her and down there between her legs, on top of her knickers, and she couldn't stop what happened then either, that she came, and he had his hand on her knickers, and he looked at her and didn't really understand and she took his hand and said that that wasn't meant to happen, she said, and she pulled up the zip on her dress. That wasn't meant to happen like that, but sometimes it does, she said, and he said that it didn't matter. And when she sat on the bus on the way home later, she had thought about David and his eyes and his face that she liked so much, and his dark grey eyes that saw everything he did. And she thought about trying to see what they saw, and that they saw totally different things from her own.

Aw, I didn't mean anything by it, David said, sitting at the table, and she looked out of the window. Of course you must meet him if you need to, he said, and she nodded. It's because he's older, he said, he's got something that I obviously don't, because he's older. I haven't got whatever it is he has, he said, and stood up. What is it that he's got that I don't? Oh, I don't know, she said. No, because I've got nothing, I've got bugger all, he said. Of course you have, she said, why are you saying that? Oh I don't know, he said. You've got so much, she said. I don't know, he said, and sat down again opposite her. And there was silence, just the sound of the doormen laughing and talking to people in the queue down below, because it was a popular place, and people waited in the queue every night in the cold and wanted to get in, and she often stood up here by the curtains and looked down at them and sometimes someone suddenly turned and looked right up at her. You've got so much that I like, she said. Yes, I guess I have, he said, and looked at her.

It's Christmas After All

THEY'RE CLOSING UP for the evening. She can see from where she's standing in her black coat, wrapped up in her shawl, looking in through the window at them closing. A misty grey snow falls over the city and she sees him empty his pint glass in there, then wrap a scarf around and button his jacket and straighten up, and then he's standing there on the step outside the pub and looking into the dark, and she watches him. He walks slowly and staggers, with stumbling, shuffling steps through the city snow, lead snow, grainy from exhaust and salt, and she follows him and breathes into her shawl. She sees him stop and look up at a window, which is brightly lit and the air smells of something, cloves, maybe roast lamb and rosemary, and she calls out after him, and it echoes and he turns, stops and stares at a taxi that's sliding down the hill. And she pushes her hair and shawl back from her face and shouts again and it echoes, and he turns and slips on the edge of the pavement and the snow, he staggers, and soon it will be night, silent night. He can't find the key to the door and he fumbles and fights with his pockets and she lifts a hand and touches his arm and he jumps. He slurs a bit, and his eyes are grainy red.

Jesus, is it you, he says, and she nods.

It is Christmas after all, Christmas Eve, she says, and she stands still, and his eyes look around her, they look over her, they take in her coat and black shawl, and she has her hands in her pockets.

Why aren't you at your mum's in the country, then, they'll be waiting for you, he says, and she leans her head

91

back and looks up at all the windows with Christmas stars in them.

Almost everyone has the same star in the window, they look almost the same, she says. Have you got a star, she says, and he's managed to get the key out of his pocket and it flashes in his hand as he opens the door, and the snow breaks free from the cloud and tumbles wet through the night, silent night, and she stands there and he stands in the doorway.

No, I don't have one, he says. Are you going to ring your mum then? Have you phoned her? It's Christmas after all, Christmas Eve.

He stands there holding the door, and her hands are cold and balled in her coat pockets.

I don't know, she says, and looks at his hand holding the door, which is broad with straight fingers.

Aha, he says, so you were about to call her and know the number.

Haven't you got it, she says.

You've got it at home, haven't you, he says, and pulls a cigarette from the breast pocket of his leather jacket and lights it. Have you dyed or done something with your hair, he says.

No, she says, and pulls the shawl down off her hair so that it uncoils and falls down on to her shoulders.

Aha, that's it, it's darker. Your hair's got darker, he says.

Yes, maybe, she says.

Well, I just went for a few beers before they closed, just a few beers because it's Christmas after all, Christmas Eve and all that, he says and she nods.

Did you call after me before, he says and she nods again and he says that he didn't hear.

Right, I didn't hear, he says.

No, she says, and he throws the cigarette past her out on to the snow on the pavement.

It's bloody freezing, isn't it, he says and she nods.

You should go home and ring then, he says and she leans back and looks up at the windows.

Which ones are yours?

Oh, it's just the one room. There's only one window looks out this way, he says.

And you've not got a star? she says.

No, I've not got one, he says.

And you haven't got a candlestick either?

No, I haven't.

Is it the kitchen that looks out this side?

Yeah, that's right, he says and wipes his hand over his mouth and chin and leaves something black behind on his jaw. Should really have shaved, he says. It's Christmas after all, Christmas Eve and all.

I've only got one room, too, she says.

Aha, right, he says. Well you'd better be getting on out to your mum's then. They'll be sitting there waiting for you with Christmas presents, he grins, and the door creaks when he opens it.

Have you lost a front tooth, she asks.

Yeah, that's right, he says, that's the way it goes. She nods.

Well, it's cold, isn't it, he says. The bus will still be running out to your mum's, won't it?

I don't know, it's a holiday, she says.

So it is, it's Christmas after all, Christmas Eve and all. He combs his hair back with his fingers. Too bloody right. I should really have cleaned up, obviously, it being Christmas I mean.

Doesn't really matter, she says, and rocks on the pavement, her feet cold in her shoes.

Oh, so it doesn't, does it, he says, and she shakes her head.

No, it doesn't matter.

Doesn't, does it, he says. So do you want to come up then? She slips on the edge of the pavement and it burns in her instep.

Jesus, watch out, it's slippery. Nice shoes you've got on, are they new?

Not really, she says.

She follows him up the stairs. Her hands are cold and balled in her pockets and the snow melts on the steps.

Hmm, right, you should have a hanger for that, shouldn't you, he says, and stands in the hall holding her coat. I'll get you a hanger, he says. It's lovely, your coat, this coat's really lovely.

It's alright, she says, and puts it over the boxes that are stacked in the hall. He picks up the beer cans and throws them into some boxes and empties the ash tray and runs around and trips and she stands there looking at a photo on the wall.

How old are you here?

What, he shouts from the kitchen, and comes in and looks at her. You're all dressed up, damn, nice clothes, damn, should've changed of course, he says.

It doesn't matter, she says.

But it's Christmas Eve after all, he says.

How old were you there, she says.

Where?

In the photo on the wall. Are you the same age as me there, she says.

I was about twenty-three, maybe, and my brother's a couple of years older, you know. Man, I haven't got much to offer you, really, he says.

Doesn't matter, she says.

Yes it does. It's Christmas Eve, after all, I should've sorted something out. He throws off his leather jacket and top and puts on a shirt, then rummages around in the wardrobe and manages to find some old blue acrylic slacks with a crease and pulls them on and she laughs.

Are those from the Seventies, she says and he grins.

Of course, this was all the rage, and he strokes back his hair and looks at her. God, you're not half like your mum, you are, he says.

94

Yeah maybe, she says.

Jesus, my brother had just the same mouth as you, crooked like yours.

Did he, she said.

Look at the picture there, and his mouth, it's exactly the same shape, the cupid's bow. Isn't that what they call it, he says, and she nods.

Do you want something to eat? You must be hungry.

It's not a problem, she says.

I bought some ham, but we ate quite a bit of it yesterday. One of the neighbours was here, Stickan from just across the way. So ham sandwiches, do you want one?

Only if you're going to have one, she says.

Of course, and do you want a beer, do you drink beer? She shakes her head.

No, it's okay, she says.

No, of course, but you'll have something to drink. Tea? Do you want tea?

Yes please, she says. He stumbles out into the kitchen and she sits down in the armchair and her hands are cold and folded on her knees.

Can I light some candles, she says.

What, he shouts from the kitchen. Candles, yes of course, we'll light some candles. It's Christmas Eve after all. He gets some candles and pushes them down into a few empty wine bottles and he sits down opposite her on the bed and cuts some ham, and every now and then he runs out into the kitchen and she hears him opening a can of beer and drinking, and when he comes back he's grinning and his eyes are shining and she feels her shoulders ache and tries to relax them.

I thought maybe you'd ring one day, she says, and looks down at his trousers, and he's forgotten to do up his flies and they're open wide.

Well, you see, they've cut off the phone. Kept going on about the bloody bills, he says, and she nods.

Before you know it. Not easy, all that, with bills, you

know, and one of Stickan's mates was living here for a while after a bust-up with the wife and he was phoning all the bloody time, like he was glued to the phone. He butters some bread and puts ham on it and chews and she sits still with her hands around the hot teacup.

Jesus, did you think I was going to call, he says, and she nods. So you went around thinking that maybe I'd call, he says, and she nods. He gets up and goes out into the kitchen and she hears him drinking and she says why doesn't he bring the beer in with him instead.

What, he shouts from the kitchen.

You can drink in here, she says, it doesn't matter. He comes and stands in the doorway with his beer.

Jesus, he says, what did you think? Did you think that, bloody Dad, he could call me sometimes? Is that what you were thinking?

Yes, she says.

So every time your phone rang, you thought that might be Dad calling. That's what you thought, he says, and she nods and looks down at her hands holding the teacup and starting to get warm. He sits down on the bed and twists the beer can, and his eyes are red.

Jesus, he says, and when it wasn't me, what did you think then?

I thought then, maybe, maybe it would be the next time, she says, and he pulls his hand through his hair, and it's trembling.

Right, yes, he grins, because you never know with Dad.

No, she says.

No, you never bloody know with Dad, he grins. She looks at him, then she looks out through the window at the night, silent night, and the snow that is falling through it.

Some Party

HE WAS GOING somewhere in the car and Lina didn't know where and she didn't ask because she didn't know if you should ask about things like that. She sat quietly in the seat beside him and outside the window there was countryside now, whereas before it had been town. And it was full summer out here in the countryside, she saw that through the windows, and the night insects splattered on the windscreen. The weather in town was nothing to write home about, with a haze of pollution that just lay there and shimmered, and she needed the toilet but she didn't know whether she should say, because he didn't seem to need it. He was driving and had said that he liked driving and she had nodded. He turned off onto a gravel track and slowed down to protect the paintwork, said that it was for the paintwork, and she nodded. They went past summer cottages and small houses, and he swung in and stopped outside some cottages, so she realised that this was where he had been heading, where he was going. And he said that she should get the wheelchair out of the boot, so she got out of the car and lifted the wheelchair out and opened it and put down the cushion and wheeled it round to the front for him, so he could get in. He pointed over the grass towards some voices that could be heard behind the house, and she pushed the wheelchair over the grass and tussocks, and he bounced around, and held on to the arms, and it was some party they were having back there, she could hear it from the voices. And when Lina went round the corner they saw him and got up and shouted.

Hey Nisse, they shouted and came over and shook him by the hand, and she stood still behind him with a firm grip on the handles. Some midges hummed over and wanted to settle, and buzzed around and got caught in her hair, and there was a caravan across the grass and a child was staring out of the window.

Was it okay driving here, and how's the leg, and the photography, are you still doing that, they clamoured.

And you've got a new motor, ay? Damn, you've got a new motor, they said, and Nisse nodded and said he certainly fucking had.

And she pushed him over to the table, because he pointed there, and she didn't know what to do with her face, which had a smile on it, and turned to look at everyone but no one acknowledged it or even noticed, so she rearranged her mouth and sat down on a chair by the table, as that was what he said she should do. And she saw that two midges were poised almost side by side on her arm, quivering, and she wasn't the sort who was greedy or stingy, so she sat and watched them and felt them feeling around with their probes and then biting. The child stared out of the caravan window and they drank from plastic glasses and kept pouring more because it was a party, after all, and they went around raising their glasses and drinking. And Nisse sat there drinking and peeling shrimps, and she watched him peeling and eating and waving away the midges and she didn't know if she should brush off his midges or if it was enough to deal with her own, but he said nothing about it.

And it was certainly some party they were having, and they staggered around in it and in the dew that fell and lay on the grass. The child stared out of the caravan at her mum who was falling about and screaming.

Leffe, for fuck's sake, she screamed, and Lina was cold and waved away the midges, and Nisse sat peeling shrimps and eating and the party lay strewn and soggy and the mum tottered into the caravan and screamed from inside.

Leffe, for fuck's sake, she screamed, and the child

came out of the caravan and stood there staring. Leffe was staggering around in the bushes, he came over the grass and sank down on a chair beside Lina.

Fuck, you've got a really nice smile. I noticed it before, Leffe said. And the child stood on the grass and saw her mother's head poking out the window and screaming.

Leffe, for fuck's sake, she screamed. And Leffe leant in towards Lina's ear.

Shit, you not going to have anything to drink, he said in her ear. Lina looked at the girl who was staring up at her mum's head hanging out and heaving and vomiting and Leffe put his arm round Lina. Of course you're going to have a beer, he said, and Lina didn't know whether she should move his arm, and she looked at Nisse who was peeling shrimps and Leffe was breathing into one of her ears and the midges were humming in the other. And the child had got hold of a hose and pulled it over and washed away her mum's puke that was dribbling down the side of the caravan and someone suddenly shouted.

Leave the nurse alone, Leffe, someone shouted, Eva it was, or maybe Susanne, and Leffe moved his arm away and Lina looked at Nisse who was peeling shrimps and eating and at the child who had finished with the hose and threw it down on the grass and ran into the caravan again. After a while, the mother's head started to loll back and forth in the window, her head fell down on the window ledge and flopped on the loose neck and then slipped down and disappeared and there was a noise from inside the caravan. Lina looked through the door and saw the child pulling her mother by the feet. And Leffe stared at Lina.

Shit, are you the nurse, he said, and Lina nodded and Leffe turned towards Nisse who was sitting peeling shrimps.

Fucking cute nurse you've got, he shouted, and Lina didn't know if she was supposed to peel the shrimps for Nisse to eat, but he hadn't said anything. Someone else came over and sat down beside her, on the other side, and smiled and looked at her and asked her about things, and they hadn't done that until now and she didn't know what she should answer. Nisse sat on his own at the end of the table and pushed shrimp shells backwards and forwards across the table and the child came out of the caravan and dragged her feet in the dew, and came over and stood beside Lina and looked at the midge that was just settling on her arm.

You've got a midge there, the girl said, and pointed at her arm and Lina nodded and the child stood watching the midge move its probe around and then finally stick it into a vein on the back of her hand. The child clung to her legs and tried to climb up onto her lap even though she was a big girl who had already started school, so she said.

And I've got a wart here, the child said and thrust the wart up into Lina's face so she could see it. The girl clambered up onto her lap and Lina looked at the wart and asked if she had more, but she didn't know if she should have asked that, and she looked at Nisse who was pushing shrimp shells across the table and down onto the grass.

Nah, I've just got one, but my friend's got four, said the child.

So you've only got one, Lina said, and the child nodded.

Yeah, why, said the child.

Because then there isn't much risk that you're a changeling, because they do that quite often, troll mums, they switch their children for human children who are not as warty and rough, Lina said, and she saw that Nisse had seen that she was talking to the child, but he said nothing about it.

Am I rough, asked the child, and Lina stroked the girl's hair that was hanging round her face, thin and tangled.

No, not especially, just a bit behind here, Lina said. Leffe had sat down beside her again and was breathing in her ear.

Fuck you're pretty, he breathed, and said to the guy who was sitting next to her, isn't she, and the guy smiled and said something to the child.

Shit, your mum's passed out in the caravan, he said to the child, and the child turned and stared at the caravan. Lina had the child on her lap and Leffe in her ear and Nisse was looking at her and stuffing a shrimp in his mouth.

Leave the nurse alone Leffe, someone shouted. Ingela maybe, or Susanne, and Leffe pulled away his arm and his mouth from her ear.

Fuck, you're the nurse, Leffe said, and the other guy asked what she earned an hour.

Sixty-seven plus overtime in the evening like now, Lina said, and Leffe stared at her and the kid stared at her wart and asked if she was sure that she wasn't a changeling.

No, of course you're not, but maybe your mum pulls out the hairs on your chin when you're asleep, Lina said.

Do troll children have hair on their chin? the girl asked.

Of course they do, Lina said, and their mouths usually smell like frogs because they like eating tadpoles.

I don't, the child said.

Have you ever tasted one, Lina said, and the child stared up her with her big grey eyes and shook her head. Lina looked at Nisse who was sitting at the end of the table peeling shrimps and eating them and turning them round in his mouth, his arms heavy on the table and his eyes heavy above them.

Come over here and I'll peel some shrimps for you, he said to the child, and the girl shook her head and picked at her wart.

You shouldn't be sitting on the nurse's knee, someone said. Maybe Eva or Susanne, or maybe it was Ingela who said that to the child, and tried to get her down, but the girl clung onto Lina's knees and screamed.

It doesn't matter, Lina said.

No, but it's Nisse who's come here to see his niece and not you, said Ingela or maybe it was Eva, or Susanne. Lina nodded and said that she obviously couldn't help it if the girl was sitting on her knee and wanted to stay there.

There was a loud crack when Nisse released the brakes on the wheelchair and rolled over the grass.

I'd thought of heading home now in any case, he said, and the child lay screaming under the table and kicked the table leg so hard that the bottles fell off and rolled around on the grass.

Now you're just tired, Ingela said to the child, or maybe it was Susanne. Lina got up and gripped the handles of the wheelchair and the others stood up and swayed.

Hope it's alright driving back, and how's the leg by the way, and the photography, are you still doing that, they said.

And you've got a new motor, ay? Shit, you've got a new motor, they said, and Nisse nodded and said he fucking well had. Lina pushed the wheelchair over the grass and he bounced around, and she pushed it up to the driver's door so he could get into the driver's seat, and then she took out the cushion and folded the wheelchair and lifted it up into the boot. She sat quietly in the seat beside him and the countryside passed outside the window, and would soon be replaced by the town.

If Only There Was a SodaStream

IT WAS A SNAKE summer. Every morning I heard Lovisa's dad whistling past the window with his boots and stick. I was woken by him walking around out there and banging his stick, and afterwards he went around the farm, past the stone mounds and a bit up the path into the woods, and then down to the summerhouse again. Monika and Stefan turned over and swore in the bedroom because, like, Jesus, you never get a lie-in, even if you practically live in the middle of nowhere. I sat up in bed and pulled up the blind and saw Lovisa's dad go past the barn and into the woods. He was wearing black wellies and a Gulf baseball cap and his neck was brown and broad underneath. And Monika and Stefan were lying in the dark of the bedroom and I stood in the doorway and looked at them but they didn't see me. I went out into the kitchen and climbed up onto the window seat, and of course Lovisa's mother was lying over there on the summerhouse lawn, sunbathing in a yellow bikini. I jumped down and got out a bowl and poured some muesli and buttermilk into it and sat down on the window seat again and ate, and looked down at Lovisa's mother lying there in her white hat, reading, and Lovisa sitting beside her.

I'm going now, I called into the dark bedroom, because they were lying there in the dark air and the sun shimmered through the gap at the bottom of the blind. I put on my wellies in the hall, because there were snakes everywhere, and I had to wear my wellies, all summer I wore them. And Lovisa's dad went around collecting snakes and chopped off their heads and threw them on the ant heap. I stood on the bottom step and below me were the snakes, everywhere they were, and I'd seen quite a few because they slithered out in the heat and lay on the gravel tracks and bathed in the sun and glistened and hissed when I cycled past. I stamped over the grass and gravel down towards the summerhouse and Lovisa's mother turned over and waved and turned the page of her *Femina* magazine, and she had blonde hair that curled down her back and smelled of hairspray. And Lovisa wasn't allowed to go until she'd eaten that piece of bread of hers, which lay big and fat on the plate, and I looked at it and Lovisa's mother smiled and turned the page and smelled of sun cream and hairspray. And I had eaten, after all, but I hadn't eaten anything like that slice of bought bread with ham, because we ate homemade in our house. Lovisa's mother lay there and turned the page and brushed some ants off her leg and I took the piece of bread and ate it.

Watch out for snakes, Lovisa's mother called after us, as we walked off in our boots, because Lovisa's mother was scared of snakes and they made her hysterical. Don't play by the stone mounds, she shouted, because it was in the stone mounds that the snakes had their nest and where they lived and lay there intertwined and cold and glistening. And every day Lovisa's dad went out in black wellies with a stick to look for snakes and chop them up with the axe and sometimes he threw them on the ant heap and we stood and watched the ants swarm around the snake and bury it and save it for winter, and every day the snake seemed to get smaller and smaller until it disappeared. And sometimes we broke off branches and stripped them and held them right on top of the ant heap, fresh and white the branches were, and the ants were curious and crawled all over them and pissed on them and sprinkled their acid and later we took the branches and licked and shook off the acid and threw them in a ditch when we'd licked them clean.

We walked in our wellies along the gravel track under

the birch trees and the sun flickered and our feet got hot and sweaty in our wellies, and I didn't think that being in wellies was good for your feet, so I took them off and carried them in my hand. The wellies hung down from my hands and were awkward and heavy so I left them standing at the side of the road somewhere, because I mean having to carry them all the time, and Lovisa took hers off too and turned round to look for her mother but she was nowhere to be seen. We walked along, side by side, our brown feet on the gravel track, and we didn't really have anything to do but we could go to see the Stockholmers and drink soda because the Stockholmers had a SodaStream and could make as much soda as you could drink. And I'd asked for a SodaStream but I hadn't got one. Bloody machines, Monika said.

But it looked like the Stockholmers weren't there. The hammock was gone and the flag, and they must have gone home and locked up the place so there wasn't any soda to be had there either. I stood and peered in through the window to see if I could see the SodaStream but couldn't see it anywhere. But we can still balance on the fence, Lovisa said, because we weren't allowed to do that otherwise.

Walking along on the hot gravel, barefoot, we didn't really have anything to do, so we looked in the ditch for a while for something but there wasn't anything to look for. Well, only a beetle that was in a hurry and beetled over the road and was busy with its own thing, and I didn't want to disturb it even though Lovisa stopped it for a while with her foot. The grasshoppers sat in the ditch and scratched their dry legs and I poked the snake skin that was lying there, drying out on the gravel, because the snakes slid up onto the road and would lay there dozing in the heat and get all drowsy and warm, lay there in the heat and slowed down and didn't manage to move quickly enough when a car came. The fields stood rustling with corn, and we weren't allowed to run in the corn either, but we could run across the meadow so we jumped over the ditch and ran across the meadow, the grass grazing our legs and bumblebees landing like hot beans. We came out by the barn and the vegetable patch and Monika was on her knees thinning the carrots. The rows of carrots were endless and the bum of her shorts stuck out between the rows and her hair hung round her neck, darkened by sweat, and the tiny carrots that had been pulled up lay shrivelling between the rows. We hunted for two big carrots and pulled them up and then ran and hid under the pump and sat on the well cover and chewed and wiggled our brown toes and saw Lovisa's mother over on the lawn, and she waved away some horseflies and turned onto her back. I threw the carrot top on the compost and followed the path down past the potato field to the plum trees, because there was shade there and it smelled sweet, and the wasps buzzed and clung to the plums and sucked from the cracks. We pulled down a branch and picked some plums and bit into the sweet flesh and spat out the stones and the sun shimmered through the leaves and the wasps buzzed loudly and lazily. And of course I saw something slithering through the grass and Lovisa saw it as well because the snake slithered up and licked her foot like a flame with its tongue and then disappeared. I let go of the branch and the plums fell heavy and swollen to the ground and she stood still and whispered that I mustn't tell her mother. Promise that you won't say anything, she whispered. I shook my head because the snake had gone, had almost never been there.

We climbed over the wall by the lawn and sat down on the well again and Lovisa was kind of shaking so I had to run and get our wellies from the road, because they were standing under the birch trees by the edge of the road, and when I got back she was sitting on the well cover and didn't feel well and rocked back and forth and Lovisa's mother was sitting on a blanket over on the summerhouse lawn putting sun cream on her shoulders and promise you won't say anything, Lovisa said, and I nodded.

We sat on the edge of well and she felt sick and got

kind of listless and wanted to lie down somewhere even though she couldn't lie down there. I walked with her down to the summerhouse and Lovisa's mother asked if anything was wrong but it was nothing, just that Lovisa was suddenly so tired and couldn't face standing up or even sitting down for that matter and it's because you've been out in the sun, Lovisa's mother said, you should really be wearing sunhats. She laid out a blanket in the shade and Lovisa dozed on it. She lay on the blanket and went numb and felt sick and I sat beside her and couldn't say anything because Lovisa's mother might get worried and hysterical, which Monika never did, but Lovisa's mother did and she came over with some water and wiped her face and Lovisa lay there dozing and couldn't even speak. You could at least answer me, Lovisa's mother said, and shook her but she just lay there and lay and dozed and couldn't do anything. I leant over to take a sneaky look at the bite on her foot and there was the bite, two red spots, and Lovisa's mother saw me and froze. I mean I was obviously looking at something else but Lovisa's mother bent down as well and looked and turned her foot and there was the bite and it was a bit swollen and red and I couldn't say anything but now her mother had seen for herself and screamed and jumped up and shouted for her dad and he came rushing from the outhouse. I sat on the blanket and watched Lovisa's dad drive the car round and drag her up from the blanket, and she hung limp in her dad's arms, and he lay her down on the backseat of the blue Volvo Amazon and Lovisa's mother sat in the front and her dad accelerated and off they drove, the exhaust pipe dangling and bumping over the grass behind them.

I put on my wellies and stamped in them on the gravel up to the farm. Monika's orange shorts were easy to see down there by the vegetable patch. And I was sure that Lovisa would get soda at the hospital because that's what my cousin said when he got concussion and went to hospital, that he'd got soda.

Ginger Cat

I

SHE WALKED DOWN the gravel track and the cats came to meet her, and they meowed and rubbed against her legs and lay down in the ditch and purred and stared. And the cottage stood there yellow and bright amongst the green firs, and she hadn't been there for a few years but she'd heard them talking about him and the cats in town, and she bent down and stroked them. Everything was silent and all she heard was her own steps on the gravel track and the apples hung heavy and sweet on the trees and the cats swarmed around her.

He had no lights on in the cottage and she stood in the doorway and couldn't see a thing.

So it's you, is it, he said from somewhere inside, and she nodded into the dark. So you're here now, he said, and she held onto the door handle and the cats darted over and rubbed against the door and her legs.

He closed the door behind her, and there were opened tins everywhere and licked-clean plates with dried cream rims and the cats sat on the worktop and in the windows they stared and meowed and he had put out chairs and footstools for them. And the cottage was small with only one room and the kitchen.

He lifted a pan out of the sink and filled it with water and turned on the stove.

We'll have some coffee then, he said, and she tried to sit down on the kitchen sofa where some cats were lying and she drove them off and they hissed. He poured water over the coffee in the filter cone.

You'll have to wash your hands before you touch

anything in here, he said, all the things you touch out there, he said. She nodded and got up, and behind her he said you never know where people have been and where they've had their hands or anything, what you've been doing and what on earth you've touched. And money, you never know where it's been and who's been touching it. She went into the bathroom and he shouted after her.

You'll see the towels there, they're hanging in order just like at home, no doubt. No doubt you've got the same system, with the first one for your face so you don't dry your hands on it, the second one for your hands, and then there's the blue one for your privates, and the cat towel is hanging there to the right, not too difficult is it? He stood outside the door talking.

You won't touch the cat towel, will you, he said, and the foot towel is in the wash, okay? She sat down on the sofa again, and the coffee was lukewarm and he stood leaning against the sink and slurped and he had no clocks and she looked surreptitiously around trying to find one. And he had a metal bucket in the corner and he stood over it and pissed in it because he had an outside loo and you can't be bothered to go out to the loo every time you need a piss, can you, or you'd just be running backwards and forwards the whole time, he said, and she nodded. His piss splattered in the bucket.

He poured some water in the bucket and opened the window and threw out the piss. Good fertiliser this, if you mix it with a bit of water. I've got hollyhocks just under the window, you probably saw them. They've never been so tall, you must have seen them and thought wow, Granddad's got some big hollyhocks there, you must have thought.

I'm not sure, she said.

You mean to say you missed the hollyhocks, you really missed them, he said, and she nodded.

Well this is a hollyhock, and they actually quite like poor bare soil. Real proletarian roses, nothing blousy about them like a bourgeois rose. You should see them in spring, makes you shiver to see them raise their heads in the flowerbed. He moved some things from the armchair and sat down.

When you were little, he said, you ran around here with the cats, right, and pulled them by the tail. Ellen left you here back then, because she worked on the tills at Konsum during the day, so I was a kind of childminder if you like. You weren't very big then, and you had to be held so you didn't fall down the hole in the outside loo. You didn't like sitting there, and you sat and looked down the hole the whole time and you had the tiniest wee bum. A bit bigger now I reckon, he said, and she nodded. She didn't remember much but she remembered the toilet now that he'd mentioned it.

You never wanted to leave when she came to get you, you wanted to stay here with Granddad and clung to me and screamed. He looked out through the window.

Well well, but you remember Bertil, don't you. Hmm? The neighbour. He always helped me with the wood but then he got a hernia and couldn't lift anything. Bertil, he died last year. So you don't remember him then? He was here all the time when his wife went a bit soft in the head and went into a home. Yes, it was a shame for poor Bertil because his wife was the quiet type, you know, always shy she was. She hardly dared look you in the eye, and then she gradually became the opposite, great long harangues and swearing that she'd been saving up for years. She became a different person. Well, I said to him, well you married her and lived with her for fifty-five years, I said. So of course you thought you knew her, I said. That's what people are like, you know. You think you know them but you've actually got no idea and it's a nightmare. He got up and walked around the room. Can you imagine the nightmare, he said, and she nodded. Uff, I've got stitches here you see, he said. Hmm? You think I've always limped and had stiff legs like this? Well, my right leg is stiff because I had to sew up my thigh here recently, I'm not usually this bloody stiff.

No of course not.

Because I managed to cut my leg you see, I hit my leg, so I had to sew it up. It was deep you know, and I stood there and looked right down into the gaping flesh. So it had to be stitched. And I certainly wasn't going to go to any bloody hospital because then they'd just keep you there for good. They'd discover a whole load of pains and ailments then, wouldn't they, and tell you it's a miracle you're alive. They bloody well examine and poke and mess about until they find a whole host of things that are wrong. Everything has to be x-rayed out of the dark you know. So, he said before continuing, and she looked around the small cottage and it was small and dirty, his cottage.

So, well, I had thread here so I stitched it up myself. I've stitched myself before, here, on my hand, I've done stitches, but it's a bit infected now and tight. Don't tell me you think I'm this decrepit and stiff all the time. You really think that? No, she didn't think anything, she hadn't thought that at all and she hadn't said anything either.

You haven't come, in all these years I've been sitting here, waiting and thinking that one day she'll come and knock on the door, he said. You're not leaving already, are you?

No, I'm not leaving. Of course I'm going to stay here now that I've come, she said, and gasped for air as there wasn't much air in the cottage.

No, then you suddenly die one night or maybe slowly over the weeks and months like Bertil did, lie there dying for several years, dying a little all the time. Not in the church, either, so you have to be buried outside the churchyard somewhere, they've probably got some ditch somewhere, and I don't pay anything to the church. But Bertil, he's got a grave up there in the churchyard, lying there in a row, a bit like terraced houses. It's a good thing he doesn't know he's lying next to Stigge, the old farmer, Stigge Eriksson. He was a twisted bastard. Every year when the wind was blowing this way you know he'd spray insecticide on the fields nearest to us. The hollyhocks would stand there like skeletons after a few days and rustle against the wall. He had a bloody mangy old dog as well that looked like it had run into a wall a few times head-on, he said. A penny for your thoughts. What are you sitting there thinking?

Nothing really, she said.

You can just sit there now, because I've got to ring Harald from the shop and order my groceries, because you order on Tuesdays, he said.

He phoned and she sat and listened and stroked some of the cats and the cats rubbed against her.

Five litres milk and four kilos fresh herring, he said into the receiver, and she looked at him sitting there on the sideboard. And then dry food, he said into the receiver, and twelve tins of Whiskas, five with cod and sardines, oh so that's been discontinued. But there's a new flavour. We haven't ordered that before. Is it good then? So you don't know what you're selling? Don't you have to know about what you're selling, or at least smell it? Can you open a tin and smell it? They think it's the smell that's most important, if it smells good it's not a problem, you see. You mean, even after I've been ordering food from you for all these years, you can't do me the service of opening a tin and smelling it, because it's too much trouble, you think that's asking too much? I see, you're sitting in the office. And listen, I noticed yesterday that you've got a new driver because he drove right up to the house. I've said before that the shopping should be left down by the post box because I take the wheelbarrow down later and pick up all the stuff because I've been doing that for years, ever since I've been ordering from you, but yesterday it was the devil himself who was driving and he drove all the way up to the yard in the van and knocked on the door and the cats were nervous. No, tell him that he should drop it down by the post box because I don't want anyone up here, not even him. Yes, of course we're nearly done, because I don't have time for this either. Do you think that I've got all the time in the world, that this is something I can spend time on? Well it's not. He put the receiver down and looked at her. That was Harald, I've made my order now, he said, and let me tell you I stood in here and saw him up-close, red hair and a baseball cap, and the cats got so nervous. I heard the van from far away and thought it's not going to drive in here and it bloody well did, right up here, he drove, and no one's driven up here for ages and no one's supposed to drive up here, and he even knocked on the door. But I was standing behind the curtains watching him, and I saw him up-close, red beard you know, and a big lump of snus under his lip, I stood here behind the curtains you know, and saw his lip.

He went over and stood by the bucket and pissed into it, then opened the window and threw out the piss.

You don't think I was rude to Harald do you? You would've heard if I wasn't nice to him.

No, I don't think so, she said.

No, you heard, I mean you were sitting here and heard what I said.

Well, I didn't really give it much thought.

When I said, so you don't know anything about what you're selling, I mean, how did that sound? And yesterday it was the devil himself, you heard me say that, and how did that sound? I mean it didn't sound very nice, is that what you think?

No, I don't really know what I think. Nothing really.

Well, it's only Harald he said, and laughed. Harald doesn't bother about little things like that, Harald, he knows me, after all, and knows that I'm alright, of course he bloody does, nothing to worry about. A short bloody conversation. After all I've been ordering from him for years he should be grateful for it, not that he's ever even offered me a single discount, nothing I've got, nothing for the fact that I've been a loyal customer, a pillar for the whole bloody business.

Maybe I should switch to Konsum, I mean every single penny he loses in those discount vouchers you cut out pains him, it actually hurts him. You'd have to look long and hard to find a more miserly bugger. And they take on people for the summer you know, with no training, who work cash in hand driving things around, and he drove right the way up here, and he certainly looked like one of their employees. The devil himself, you heard what I said. Do you think it wasn't very nice? Because he'll talk to the others, like Solveig in the butchers. No, you know what? I should call and talk to him again, you know, hear what he's got to say, but then he'll start to wonder why I've called him again. You can't just keep ringing all the time.

No, she said.

But some things need to be sorted out, I mean, the fact that I said the devil himself drove up was maybe a bit unnecessary, I mean, I could explain that today's been a difficult day, you see, and I took it out on him. I'm in a lot of pain, you see, since the stitches, and it makes you a bit tetchy. So you don't think I was unfriendly then, he said, and she shook her head.

But it was earlier in the conversation that I said so you don't know anything about what you're selling. I assume you remember that clearly, he said.

Yes, I remember, she said.

So, that might be seen as a bit aggressive, but it was really only a question and not an attack, you understand, and I think it's interesting to know how they work in the shop, you know, purely objectively, and if things taste nice or not.

But it's nothing to worry about really, she said.

So you think I'm worrying about it, do you? That I've got time to worry about things like that? Then you don't know me, he said.

No, no, she said, I didn't mean that, that's not what I said either. There was silence. And they sat there in silence

115

and she stroked a cat that was on the kitchen sofa and it wasn't actually completely silent. She heard sounds in the silence and he seemed to hear them too. He crept over and looked out from behind the curtain. Yes, they're there again see, he said, and she went over and stood beside him and looked out and saw that there were some kids climbing up on the roof. He opened the window and shouted, get down from there you little buggers, you get down off that roof double quick and not a single tile better be out of place because then I'll skelp the lot of you go, he shouted, and she saw them jumping and sliding and slipping off the roof and running away. Yes, go on, run, and don't come back and climb on that roof again, I know how many tiles I've had to replace. Damn, they were frightened, disappeared just like that, and scarpered across the fields. Did you see them run? They nearly fell off the roof, jumped, and it's high to jump down from there, you know. He leant out of the window.

Is that a sandal? So he lost a sandal, the little one. Look, the little one with the white hair lost his sandal. It's lying there on the ground, the sandal. It's a little sandal that you can hardly see it it's so small, he said, he had such small feet that little boy. Yes, very small feet. Well, it can't just be left to lie there. Just lie there like rubbish. What will people think when there's sandals lying all over the place, making a mess. People think all sorts of things.

Yes, that's right, she said.

Better go out and get it later then. You had small feet like that, once, but they're big now aren't they, your feet, he said. She sat in the sofa and looked at his yellow jowly face and his bright eyes.

That's right, as soon as you're born you start to die, and then you die slowly throughout your life, but you don't notice it until you're old.

You see that cat on the roof, he said, and she stretched over and looked out.

The ginger stripy one, can you see him. He's been lying there all day, he likes lying there, you see, on the roofing

116

felt because it gets warm, he said, and she leant towards the window sill and saw the cat lying there blinking and twitching its ears, ginger paws lolling over the edge. The cat lay there, bright ginger against the black felt.

As soon as you get near him he's off into the woods. And he's got really big, see, look at his haunches, and he's a right one for playing high and mighty, that one.

He had a gun on the wall that he took down and turned and inspected. I don't shoot elk, never have really, but Bertil, he hunted elk. But you have to thin them out every now and then, shoot and thin 'em out, he said, and opened the window. That one there nearly killed one of the young males the other day. He pointed the gun out of the window.

He's disturbing the family, that one, and it's a fine family that I've got, but he frightens the other males away, and every litter born this spring has been ginger. There's good meat on that one. He's no more than four years either. He bent down and aimed.

So you're going to shoot him, she said, and gasped for air.

He's been lying there and relaxing on the roofing felt for long enough, he said, and fired. The shot exploded and she jumped. And that's what they said back in the town. That he shot things. She'd heard them, because the kids had heard shots and dug up cat skulls. She'd heard that the kids had found cat skulls with bullet holes.

Now you'll see how big the bastard is, he said, and disappeared out the door and she saw him wading through the grass.

It was getting dark and he'd taken off his work trousers and put on some good black trousers and a white shirt.

It's evening, after all, and I've got a visitor, he said, and lit a candle. She was gasping for air and wondered if she could open the window.

No, for god's sake don't do that, the midges will get in.

He sat in the armchair and the candle on the table was between them.

Yes well, he said, and she nodded and he had white foam in the corners of his mouth that wasn't there before.

Would you, because I've been thinking about the cats recently you see, would you look after them, he said, and she nodded. You could maybe sell some. I'll shoot some as well but there are some that I usually keep in here. You could maybe take a few home with you, just a couple, I mean, just a few. Can you look after the cats, could you do that for me, he said, and she nodded.

II

She walked into the kitchen and Ellen was sitting there doing the crossword.

They called from the shop, Ellen said. Because he obviously hadn't ordered food like he usually does.

He hadn't, she said.

So they'd started to wonder down at the shop, and Harald was obviously worried when he didn't answer the phone, so they'd gone out there. But we should have some coffee, shouldn't we, Ellen said, and got up to make it.

Because he drank a lot of coffee, he liked it, Ellen said. It was that man Harald who called, Ellen said, and blew on her coffee, because they'd been out there and knocked on the door and gone in because it obviously wasn't locked. She put a spoon in the mug and stirred.

Did you notice anything different about him when you were there? I mean, you were the last one there.

No, he was just like normal.

He was just like normal, Ellen said.

Right then. I know how he was.

The cats slunk out when they opened the door, and they'd obviously been stuck in there for a long time, she said. It's a shame that we don't have anything to go with the coffee, something to nibble.

Yes, she said.

He was sitting in the armchair, Ellen said, he always liked those armchairs, and he got them cheap, you know, they were reduced. He always told you what a bargain he'd got with those armchairs and how much he'd saved on them because they were quality. And they certainly bloody lasted, but we'll have to throw them out now. She sipped her coffee.

And what about the cats?

They snuck out straight away, the cats. They'll manage, cats are tough, but they were a bit thin. They were fat enough before, I tell you. And the taps drip in the kitchen so they had water.

So you think they had water, she said, and sat down.

Yes, of course they had water, Ellen said. And Harald said there was a fair stink, as he'd been sitting in the armchair for several weeks. I think we can just chuck them now. He had his good clothes on, he wanted them on, I guess, maybe he felt it.

Yes, maybe he did.

They said we'll have to just get rid of everything because the smell lingers, you know, you can't get rid of it. There wasn't much left of him either, obviously, as he'd been sitting there so long, so not much left. It wasn't easy to recognise him properly because, well, the cats, they hadn't been given any food you see.

But they were alive.

Yes, they were alive, Ellen said, but they had obviously been at him and eaten bits. She looked at her nails and picked under them. Well, it looked like he'd just gone to sleep. They said there's loads of bloody cats out there.

What are we going to do with the cats, then? Are we going to take them, she said.

No bloody way are we taking them. They're so horrible. They sit there and yawn tuna fish and rub their backsides on the furniture and everything, and they rub against your legs, it's horrible. And you have to lift them up all the time because they can't be bothered to jump.

But they came down the road to meet me when I went, she said.

I'm surprised they could be bothered to walk that far. Were they fat, Ellen said.

Yes, of course they were fat.

So they were out of breath then, the cats, from having walked that far, were they, Ellen said. But he must've been glad that you came. He'd been waiting a long time for that.

We could maybe have some of them here, couldn't we, and then we could sell some, if we put an advert in the paper. We could sell some of the young ones.

Yes, but you realise it costs money to put in an advert, Ellen said, every word costs.

But we could make up the money if we sold some.

Hmm, you're right, that's smart thinking actually.

Black Hole

YOU COULD SLIP in the bath if you didn't stand properly and you had to stand still and the water heater could only hold as much as it held before the water went cold and it took a long time to heat up again. And Dad soaped her down thoroughly because it was important to wash properly, all over, and in all places, otherwise there was a risk of eczema and other things flaring up and starting to itch, so she put her hands against the tiles because you could slip. And it was specially important to be thorough down there and when it was time to wash there he said that you need to keep your balance so you don't slip and knock the back of your head because that's what her cousin had done, he had fainted and disappeared, and she had asked him, well where he was when he wasn't there, but he didn't know because he couldn't remember it at all. His fingers looked funny when they came from behind and peeked out from down there, and washed and soaped, and it got warm as well and kind of tickly. And you couldn't let the water run when you were washing because then it ran and you wasted it and then there was only cold water when you wanted to rinse off the soap. And the shower was temperamental because just when he had turned it on and got the right temperature it got too hot and started to steam and burn and it was a stupid shower and rubbish, he said, and started to turn the taps again and the sweat gathered and dripped off his brow. The soap smelt sweet and steamy and foamy and his fingers peeked out from down there and she stood leaning against the tiles with her hands because her cousin had had no support and he couldn't remember anything when she asked and was allowed to touch the bump under his baseball cap with Iron Maiden on it. And the fingers washed and rubbed because the soap, you had to be thorough with the soap, and the fingers were moving fast down there, shaking legs and trembling and the soap foamed and smelled so sweet. And her legs gave way and trembled and the foam ran, the fingers rubbed and jumped, and her tummy went heavy and soft, and the darkness came from her tummy and the heaviness came over her, so her legs gave way and went soft, and she sank down into the black hole that just sucked and swallowed her up.

That's How Things Should Be

THE AUGUST HEAT billowed in the curtains and the material that Elina had tried to hang in front of the window, and the air conditioning system hummed out in the courtyard, and wherever she went, there were things and clothes and chairs. Jakob stirred on the sofa bed and she could have lain down next to him, but now she was up and looked through the crack in the door to the next room at Johanna and Måns with their deep steady breathing, because they were asleep and hadn't thought of waking. She stood and looked at them and at Jakob and walked back and forth across the floor and her hair hung long and warm down her back and itched, and she should wash it because it was itching now, and Jakob stirred and would soon wake up, no doubt, and feel around for his glasses, and she was hungry because there still wasn't enough food and she needed more. And they really should wake each other up now but they didn't because they were still asleep.

She stepped into the shower and stood, leaning forward, as she wetted and shampooed and rinsed her hair and her hair was thick and dirty and the shower cabinet rocked and her elbows hit the wall and the sweat poured down her neck and someone knocked on the door and wanted to get in and she twisted the water out of her hair. And when she came out, Jakob was sitting on the bed, scratching himself, and was awake and she looked at him and he was nearly naked and she said they're sleeping, but he said that they could wake them. And he was sweaty and warm and flushed and went out into the bathroom to have a shower, and she followed and stood by the door and the door creaked when she pushed it open, and he didn't like her standing there

123

watching, but she liked it and the window to the courtyard was open and the birds sang and the curtain was thin and light and trembled and the sun shone in. And he took off his pants and the shower cabinet knocked and rocked as he got in and he was warm and sweaty in there, and she wanted to reach out her hand to him but she stood in the doorway, and it creaked and he didn't really like her standing there.

A ball bouncing in the courtyard, voices from the neighbours, curtains billowing in the heat and the sun. Johanna sipped her coffee, and her silver-painted toenails shone under the table, her foot against the table leg, and again and again the cups clattered and Måns sat reading the map. The ventilation hummed and the birds sang. They had woken her this morning with their scavenging from the overfull bins down there. And they were going to rent a car and go somewhere, and they hovered over the map and pointed and planned, and Elina ate apricots, warm, small and hairy, and spat the stones out, down onto the street. Johanna came out to smoke and pointed and turned the map and pointed at places and roads and it was hot on the balcony and the concrete flayed the soles of their feet. And the evening before, they had sat here at the table and she had thought that now, finally, I'm sitting here in Paris, so now I just want to be able to sit here, and she had simply sat there and drunk wine and the others had sat with her and drunk wine because they had sat there, all four, and she had sat there with them.

Later she sat in the rented car, and she had on her sandals and she had clips in her hair and she sat there and things were just as they should be, with her dress above the knees and her hands clasped on her lap, and she didn't know where they were going, only that they were going somewhere, now, so she could sit in the back with her feet in sandals and they were brown, both her legs and her feet. Johanna sat beside her, smoking, and Jakob's neck was in front of her, and she liked touching it, but not when others were watching. And she didn't talk much, she really didn't, but was quiet, and sometimes she could talk lots with Jakob, sometimes sit and chat and the words just came one after the other and he listened to them. But she was sitting in the back of the rented car that smelt of plastic and outside was the French countryside and gardens and villages. And obviously they were on their way to Normandy because that was where everyone went when it was as warm as this, then everyone went there, and she looked out through the window and she looked at Jakob's neck in front of her and she wanted to lean forwards and smell it. But Johanna was sitting beside her and smoking and leaning forwards over Måns and the map and pointing and chatting away. Soon they would see the sea, Johanna said, and pointed and showed her on the map and smoked and her Swedish was a bit rusty and cumbersome after having spoken something else for so many years. Johanna handed her the water bottle and her bracelets jangled.

Jakob parked outside a large casino and there ahead of them, beyond the casino, was the sea, and they walked over the car park towards the swimming pool and the hotel and the bouncy castle, where children jumped up and down and screamed, and on the beach the children ran around with plastic kites that fluttered and spluttered and there was the sea, and sun and kites that fluttered and dived the whole time, and those small dip-backed ponies that walked around the enclosure with children on their back and sneered under their forelocks and bared their yellow teeth, ponies walking round and round with children on their backs, and the children sat on their backs, legs dangling. Johanna laid the blanket out on the sand and Elina sat on it and something crackled out of the loudspeaker across the beach and the kites fluttered and disappeared. And the beach was full of parasols and children and bathing huts all in a row. Jakob sat and looked out to sea and she looked at him and his hands, those warm dry hands he had, lying there big on the blanket. And sometimes she wanted to take his hands and hold them but now they were just lying there on the blanket where he'd put them, and he lifted one hand and pointed and said something and she liked his hands, and when they touched her, but now they were just lying there on the blanket where he'd put them, and she looked at them and here she was sitting on a beach in Normandy, and the plastic kites fluttered and dived and the children ran around and sprayed sand on the blanket and Johanna smoked and took some apricots and bananas out of the rucksack and the ponies walked in circles with the children on their back and thought about something else and the parents stood waiting outside the fence and watched and the sun came out and it was hot and then it disappeared again.

She squashed an apricot against the roof of her mouth and spat the stone out onto the sand and Johanna and Måns went down to swim, and the kites fluttered and it was hot, but here by the water there was a breeze, and she saw Måns and Johanna wading by the water's edge, the waves breaking against them, and Johanna's bikini was bright red and Jakob said that it was good for the soul to look at the horizon and she saw Måns and Johanna lose their balance and hold on to each other in the water, and the waves and the breeze, and she asked Jakob who had said that about the horizon, and he couldn't remember. Some plastic kites came flying down nearby and sprayed them with sand and she brushed it off and looked at Måns' and Johanna's heads bobbing up and down in the water and disappearing then reappearing again. She squeezed the apricots that were overripe and soft and Måns and Johanna came back across the sand towards her with the water running off them and the red bikini. Johanna rummaged around for a cigarette and the water was obviously warm and Johanna wrung the water out of her hair and there was orange peel and rubbish and Coke cans on the sand, and every now and then a voice would bark something out from the loudspeaker, across the beach and the sea and the parasols that stood swaying all in a row.

She got up and walked across the sand and where are you going, Jakob asked, and she walked and looked for the toilets in the pool building. There were several small cubicles in the toilets and she went into the one furthest in, and the sun flickered through the grille on the window high up on the wall, and she could hear the flags flapping and children shouting and the waves, and she pulled up her dress and put her hand down her pants and touched herself there with her hand, stood there and touched herself. And she stood and looked at the sun flickering through the grille on the window and she had her hand inside the material. Her hand snuck in and she touched herself with it, and leant against the wall and her breathing was totally silent and her hand, and she heard someone pee in the cubicle beside her and pull the paper, and her legs trembled, and her breathing, and the hand down there moving.

Afterwards she stood outside the cubicles and washed her hands and looked at herself in the mirror and brushed her hair into place across her forehead and her cheeks were flushed. And outside there was sunlight and sand, and she walked slowly across it. Johanna turned and saw her and waved. There was Johanna, and she waved back, and walked in between all the people running and playing beach ping-pong and the children with their kites and the ones lying there sunbathing and putting on sun cream, and on she walked because she was in Normandy now, and she had never been there before but she was there now, and Johanna waved and she waved back and brushed her hair away from her face.

She stayed a few steps behind the others as they walked down all the alleys and stopped at every restaurant and looked at the menu and peered into the restaurant. She walked a bit behind them, and her hair blew in her face as the sea was nearby and the breeze blew down the alleys and the sun had left its warmth in her face, which was flushed, and they wandered along looking and reading the menus. Jakob turned round and her hair blew in her face the whole time, the breeze on her face, and Jakob turned and she wanted to touch and hold his hands now, when they were walking, but they never walked and held hands because holding hands was something that other people did, as if they couldn't walk on their own and had to hold each other up. Sometimes she took his hands and did all kinds of things with them, but now she walked behind Jakob and they went into some restaurant and stood there and the waiter came over in a dirty apron, he came over, and they sat down and there were hardly any other guests in the restaurant but there was a little white dog sitting there, staring, and it was fat and the waiter patted the dog on the head and they were about to order and choose something from everything you could choose from, so she sat there choosing and the waiter scratched the dog and wondered if they would like a Calvados because he was offering one on the house and of course they wanted one and the waiter, he wasn't really walking straight, and kind of sloped off to get the Calvados and came back with glasses sparkling on a tray that was dirty and yellow, and they stood upright but the liquid splashed and he put them down and dried his hands on his apron and patted the dog that was sitting there, staring. And Johanna smoked and the dog stared at the Calvados whenever they took a sip. And what was it with the waiter? He winked at her and smiled at her, and she turned away because he was smiling at her and why would he smile at her and wink? Johanna smoked and picked at her starter, her shoulders red from the sun and the vest cutting into her skin, and she was hungry, that constant hunger, and Jakob sat beside her, his slow movements right next to her. The waiter came out with the food and he'd got something red on his apron and grinned and stood there and wiped something red from his hands on the apron and asked if they would like some more Calvados because it was on the house, he told them, and he was chewing on something and they certainly wanted more Calvados and the dog stared at the food and jumped up onto the sofa beside her and the waiter scratched the dog and stood there swaying ever so slightly and the dog stared at the food and didn't give up. The breeze had played with her hair and tangled it and she tidied it with her fingers and things were as they should be, and Johanna lit a cigarette and savoured the Calvados and Måns was going to drive back so he wasn't drinking any Calvados so the others drank his undrunk glass, and suddenly an ambulance or something with a siren came driving down the alley, the siren wailing and flashing, and the waiter and the cook came running out from the kitchen and looked out of the door and ran after the ambulance in their clattering clogs and the dog jumped down and ran after them. Johanna grinned and smoked and people came out into the alley and looked and ran along. And it didn't really taste of anything, the fish that was lying on her plate, it tasted of nothing, really, but she was so hungry all the time, like something was empty, and she drank the Calvados and her cheeks were flushed by it and the sun, and her hair tumbled, tangled and long. And the white dog came running in through the door again and up onto the cushion beside her, panting, and the cook came next and the waiter's clogs clacked and the cook puffed and wiped his brow and disappeared into the kitchen. And she sat there and ate the fish although it didn't really taste of much at all and Johanna smoked and the waiter came out with the tray again and the golden Calvados glasses stood there shining and sparkling and the waiter tottered over and put down some sticky glasses then offered them some more Calvados, he did, and he grinned and the dog sat there all white and fat and he had no business in the kitchen, the waiter, because he stood in the doorway and watched and grinned and Elina drank the Calvados and the heat and yellow ran down inside her.

She got up and felt the Calvados and it made her sway and she made her way out into the alley behind the others. She walked through the alleyways to the car, and the dark lay soft and warm over everything and the Calvados lay heavy and hot.

She sat there in the dark in the back of the car with the

Calvados and it made her drowsy and Måns was driving and put on some music and she drowsed and dropped off and Måns turned up the music and said you're not falling asleep are you, and Jakob was sitting in front and she looked at his neck and the hair that climbed it into a peak, and his neck was red from the sun, and warm, his neck.

It was late by the time they were sitting in the flat and drinking wine, and the air conditioning system hummed in the courtyard and Johanna stood smoking on the balcony. Elina smoothed her dress over her knees and now she was actually in Paris, and she had never been here before, but she was sitting here, now, and Jakob was sitting opposite.

Viviann Sabina

HIER, HERE, NADIA's stepfather shouted to the dog but the dog didn't come. It ran around, sniffing everywhere between the houses, even though her stepfather stood and shouted *hier*, here, on the lawn, shouting, and Emma was lying on one of the sun loungers and looked up at the stepfather's brown round belly that he was displaying to the sun and the neighbours. And beside her sat Nadia with the pigeon they'd found and were trying to feed, but it didn't seem to have any appetite, just sat on her shoulder and pecked at her pink plastic earring, and it was summer and Emma was at the villa in Germany and Nadia's mother Viviann lay dozing in the shadows, her eyelids heavy with red wine and mascara, and she had this perfume, and Viviann lay there giving off her smell and her chest rose and fell and was alive under her tunic, because that's where they were and where they lived, and her necklace hung and jangled between them, and she had warm hands and arms that she hugged with, and short strong fingers with rings that she rolled cigarettes with. Emma lay in one of the sun loungers and Viviann lay in the other and smoked and dozed and was there, and the stepfather shouted to the dog, *hier*, here, he shouted, and the lost pigeon sat on Nadia's shoulder and didn't have an appetite.

In the evening, Viviann stood in the kitchen and made food and drank wine, and her teeth were red from wine and lipstick. Later, they sat down at the long table and drank wine from large glasses, and they didn't drink red wine at home, and if they did, Emma wouldn't have got any anyway. But there she was, drinking red wine, and Viviann leant over and said *Du hast schöne hände*[5], Emma, and she leant over and said it, and Emma looked down at her hands, and always, she'd hated them. And Vivann ate and sat there and just ate and sighed and looked around the table and took her time and enjoyed it, and the dog lay under the table and you could warm your feet on it, because the dog was lying under the table and it was warm and licked up the crumbs. And in the evening the stepfather sat and warmed the hash, then rolled a joint and smoked, and Viviann and the stepfather lay on the cushions and smoked and played cards and Emma sat there on some cushions as well, with Nadia, and the stepfather rolled another and handed it to them, and Emma didn't have a stepdad either, just a real dad, who was tall and thin and smelt of snus, but Nadia had a stepfather with a black beard that was shiny and long and who whispered to Viviann soft and deep. Though later he'd become a *scheiss*, the stepdad, right now he wasn't a shit, and he lay there and smoked and dozed and talked in a soft deep voice and Viviann stroked his belly that stuck out and was brown. And Emma hadn't smoked much of the stuff before, but now she was sitting there, smoking in the villa, and playing cards and the pigeon was lying in a box and panting and looking all over the place. And Viviann had a slowness to her words and body and moved slowly and put her cards on the table and the stepfather lay there on the cushions and smoked, and he wasn't a *scheiss* then, but later he would be, and would carry on with that woman at work and demand money from Viviann because he'd paid for her and entertained her for all those years, and long after she'd moved he would phone her and say that, and shout on the answering machine in a completely different voice, because he wasn't being a *scheiss* now, when he was lying there on the cushions with Viviann, and the dog lay beside them and *hier*, here, he'd shouted at it, but it hadn't come. And he had small square hands with which he laid out the cards,

5. You have beautiful hands.

and brown eyes that squinted behind the smoke, and you couldn't see anywhere that he had *scheiss* in him that would germinate and grow and throw bottles and push Vivian's big warm body against sharp objects. Because now Viviann was lying there with the stepfather and stroking his brown belly and he stroked her long red hair and twisted it round his fingers and hand and Viviann had dark red lips that slowly released the cigarette and blew out the smoke. She had slow fingers that took their time over things, over those special places, and Emma's mum wasn't like that at all, but was a sharp and efficient mother who was always busy somewhere else. And Emma lay there on the cushions and had a smoke and Vivianne stroked her hair, her hand over her hair, and she leant forwards and said *Du hast schöne hände,* Emma, and Emma didn't see her hands in the same way as before, after that. Emma didn't have a mother who looked at other people's hands and things, and who dozed and fell asleep and lay around, and was just there.

At the villa at night Nadia and Emma slept on separate mattresses in the back room, and sometimes there were sounds at night, sometimes she heard Viviann on the stairs, soft and slow on the stairs, and noises from the bedroom, different noises from the bedroom and the stairs, when Viviann went up or down. Because Viviann lived in the villa then, and in the morning she opened the terrace door and the dog ran out and the stepfather shouted *hier,* here, after it in his soft deep voice and Viviann sat there on the terrace and sunned her legs and drank coffee with warm milk and had her first smoke. But later when the stepfather had turned into a *scheiss* she would move into a flat instead, which was noisy and dark, and Viviann trod heavy on the stairs and there was no lift and you could smell the neighbour's cooking in the bedroom and hall. Nadia and Emma would sit there on the white fitted carpet and smoke Viviann's hash, and Viviann didn't have a TV but she had hash, and they sat there and smoked and she was still the same Viviann, but not quite the same as before, because she was thin and lived in a flat that smelt of the neighbour's cooking, but she wasn't like that now, and right now she sat on the terrace and ate breakfast *brötchen* and her toes shone and smelled newly varnished and red and the stepfather shouted *hier,* here, to the dog that ran around sniffing everywhere. Nadia and Emma squinted and sat on the terrace amongst all the houses and ate *brötchen* and marmalade, and Emma didn't normally eat white bread for breakfast because it was usually rye meal porridge at home, in Sweden, that she stood and made in the morning with jam.

Nadia sat with the lost pigeon and tried to feed it with soaked bread but it pecked and blinked and had no appetite and the stepfather sat there with his pipe and brown belly in the morning sun because he wasn't a *scheiss* then, the *scheiss* was lying hidden somewhere inside, and you couldn't see it. And Viviann lay on the sun lounger and sighed and smoked because she was healthy and lay there enjoying it, though later she would get ill and walk heavily on the stairs outside the flat, and that was where she would later sit in the kitchen and smoke and was ill, and Nadia and Emma sat there and ate pasta in all the smoke and looked out into the courtyard and the rubbish bins. They sat there and smoked and drank red wine and ate pasta and Viviann was silent and tired and sat there twisting her rings and the neighbour was frying something that stank out the hall.

But it wasn't like that now, anyway. Now she got up from the sun lounger and said that she wanted to go to the woods, and she had lipstick on her teeth and her hair was red and newly washed and soft. So they went to the woods in the stepfather's big Audi and walked the dog there, and Emma wasn't used to woods like this, that weren't forests, but more like some kind of hall with pillars and a floor you could walk on, and she'd never walked this way, in this kind of wood, with a shimmering roof that flickered green when she looked up. They had pine forests at home, all stony and dark. The dog ran around, sniffing everywhere, and the stepfather held Viviann by the hand and Viviann had her hand in his, and she had a shawl on her shoulders and her hair fell red and curly over it, and high up there, the leaves stood and swayed and whispered and underneath the ground was damp and cool. And *hier*, here, the stepfather shouted to the dog, which was black and fast, and Emma didn't have a dog at home and wasn't used to them, as they only had a cat that always lay on top of the fridge and ate anything. And Viviann walked in the woods and the stepfather held her hand and she held his and it was later, one time, when she was getting dressed that she felt the lump, and she hadn't had a lump before that stayed, and was hard and round, but this lump stayed and she went around feeling it. And the lump sat there, and she could feel it, and it grew and sometimes she forgot, because everyone has lumps somewhere if you look for them. But then the lump started to take over everything, took and took, and she couldn't do anything because of the lump, and it took everything and she got thinner and went to the doctor with the lump, because it stuck to her, and she carried it around. And then she sat in the flat and waited for the results from the doctor and was alone, but she had the lump that she could feel.

But she didn't have a lump to touch now, when she was walking in the woods, and she touched the stepfather's hand, and held it as she walked. Big and warm she was, under her tunic, and the stepfather held her hand faithfully, and even though he was holding her hand it wasn't like a *scheiss* would do, because they have sweaty, limp hands, not at all like the one holding hers. He wasn't walking around with a wet fish hand like a *scheiss,* because the *scheiss* was slumbering, and only later would it wake up and grow. And suddenly the woods finished and the stepfather's big Audi stood there shining, and Emma wasn't used to woods finishing just when they had started, because the forests at home were never-ending, even though they thinned out a bit. The stepfather let the dog into the car and Emma and Nadia sat in the back and Viviann smoked in the front seat and turned on Barbra Streisand. And the stepfather sat and drove at one hundred and forty on the autobahn, and Viviann pulled down the sun visor and put her lipstick on in the mirror, and Emma had never driven at a hundred and forty before, and her dad didn't like cars, and mostly cycled around with those brown panniers that bounced around on the back. But Nadia's stepfather, he drove at one hundred and forty, and he had his brown hands on the wheel and Vivann hummed along to Streisand and put on purple lipstick and the stepfather took one brown hand off the wheel and stroked Viviann's thigh with it.

And in the evening, women came to the house because Viviann ran courses in yoga and meditation. Here they came, and they filled the hall with sandals and cardigans, and the stepfather sat somewhere else because then it was the women, and Viviann stood in the hall and welcomed them and her necklace glittered and jittered between her breasts, because they were swinging in there, and alive and big and warm. The women sat round in a circle up in the attic, on a blue fitted carpet, their legs crossed, and Nadia and Emma sat there too and closed their eyes and listened to Viviann's voice, which was slow and calm. The women came there in the evening and filled the hall and the house with their voices and smells, but they were missing later, in the flat, because there wasn't room for any women, but now Viviann stood there in the evening and welcomed the women, and when they'd gone she made food because Viviann liked food. She cooked and tasted and stirred and her breasts swung heavy and brown under her tunic and her hair curled red over them and she didn't have a lump, either, but later it would come, the lump, and she would get sick leave and sit there in the flat with the lump and with the test results that lay there, scrawled and black on the white paper. And Viviann walked heavily on the stairs, and she went to the doctor and sat there and felt sick and was pale from the radiotherapy and pills, and Nadia came and cleaned and carried bags and sat with Viviann in the kitchen and talked about the stepfather who was a *scheiss* and demanding money from her and writing letters all the time, they got letters, and she couldn't face opening them. And Emma came to the flat sometimes and sat with Nadia and Viviann and ate pasta, and when Viviann had gone for a rest they sat on the white fitted carpet and smoked Viviann's hash before going to that Hard Rock place and standing there and head-banging in the dark, amongst all the other hair. And when they got back, Viviann was sleeping, and Viviann didn't have hair anymore, not then, just thin wisps that trembled on the pillow, not at all like now, when she stood there by the stove in the villa, cooking chicken, and stirred and tasted. Because now her hair was thick and red and smelt of henna, and the dog lay on the floor and licked her toes and chewed on whatever she dropped. And in a box on the shelf lay the lost pigeon which panted and stared, and Nadia tried to feed it with crumbs and seeds. And they sat there, around the table, and ate Viviann's food and drank wine and the women had left their scents and voices in the house and Viviann talked about them and the dog lay under the table and Emma warmed her feet on it and Viviann leant over the table and said *Du hast schöne hände* Emma, she said, and Emma looked at her hands because Viviann sat there and leant over and looked at her hands and she couldn't hide them.

But later Viviann would sit there in the flat in the evenings and touch the place where her breast had been, and the lump, and wait for a new one to appear. And Nadia phoned sometimes and dropped by to find out how things were and it was always more or less the same, although Viviann had started to work again so didn't always sit there in the kitchen and smoke and play Patience, but she often did, and Nadia had her own flat and a boyfriend so she couldn't go there all the time, in the evenings, but sometimes she did, and sat in the kitchen and talked about the stepfather who was a *scheiss* and had got a lawyer involved. And Nadia was studying and had a boyfriend, so she wasn't there all the time, to know what was going on. And then one day they called from Viviann's job and wondered where Viviann was, but Nadia didn't know and didn't keep tabs on her, and the people from her work just wondered, because she should have been at work but she wasn't, and she wasn't answering the phone, either. And Viviann could be anywhere, so Nadia sat there, and phoned Viviann's friends, but they didn't know anything. So Nadia got on the tram with Viviann's key in her pocket and her hand clenched round it. And she went into the shop on the way and bought some bread and yoghurt and fruit for Viviann, because Viviann was no doubt in bed and was tired and ill and would want something. And Nadia walked along Viviann's street and through the entrance and across the yard. It smelt of food on the stairs and Nadia stood outside the door and knocked and rang the bell, but nothing could be heard from inside, and she had the key in her hand, after all, she had it, and she opened the door and there in the hall was the smell of Viviann's cigarettes and the neighbour's cooking, and she looked at herself in the mirror on the wall and smoothed her newly-cut fringe, which curled on her forehead, and Viviann's things were all over the place in the hall, hanging there, all the photos and scarves and candlesticks on the wall, and the glass lampshade on the ceiling chimed in the draught from the door when she closed it. She went into the kitchen and ran the tap and stood there and drank some water, and the washing up was piled up and mouldy and it smelled a bit, because Viviann didn't like washing up, never had, though she was good at stacking the dishes, and there was the ashtray by the window that Nadia had made at school with Viviann's lipstick-red stubs in it. She stood in the doorway to the sitting room, and the reading lamp was on and hanging over the armchair because that was where she always sat and read and dozed and smoked, and she must have forgotten to turn it off, and the door to the bedroom was ajar and Viviann's sheepskin slippers were outside and Nadia went over and opened the door. And there she was, lying on the bed, and Nadia shouted that you have to wake up now, Mum, and phone your work, and she had bought some bananas and bread but Viviann just lay there, completely still, far too still she lay there, with her mouth slightly open. Her arm was hanging over the side of the bed and Nadia went over and lifted it up and her arm was cold and rigid and she screamed and grabbed hold of her mother and hugged her and shook her and hugged her and a noise came out of Viviann, gurgled out of her, but then there was no more.

But that wasn't now, that was much later, because now Viviann sat there and was warm and alive and present, and leant over the table and smiled and had lipstick on her teeth, and the dog licked her toes under the table, and she stretched over and filled Emma's wine glass and the stepfather raised his glass to the cook, to Viviann Sabina, and Emma's mother didn't have a name like that at all, but had something short and Finnish that she used. And the dog lay under the table and licked Viviann's feet. It licked her toes and she giggled and brushed her red hair out of her face and looked around the table and drank. And the terrace door stood open to the summer, and to the houses, and the dog stood in the doorway and sniffed and slunk out and *hier,* here, shouted the stepfather to the dog, but it didn't come back.

And later, the flat stood empty, and just stood there, and then Nadia came with her things and moved in, because she wanted to be where Viviann had been, and walk where she had walked, and Emma helped and carried her things and tidied. And Emma wouldn't have made her bed exactly where Viviann's had been, she would have put it somewhere else, but Nadia pulled her fringe down over her forehead and wanted her bed where Viviann's had been. Afterwards they sat in the kitchen and looked out into the yard and smoked, and Nadia stubbed out her lipstick-red filters in the ashtray and drank wine, and Emma lifted her glass and looked at her hands.

About the Author

One of Sweden's most exciting young female writers, **Mirja Unge** was born in 1973. She received the Katapult Award for her critically acclaimed first novel, *Det var ur munnarna orden kom* [*Out of Your Mouth the Words Come*], 1998, and in 2000 she published *Järnnätter* [*Anticlockwise*]. The same year her novel *Motsols* [*Tide*] was shortlisted for the Swedish Radio Award. Amongst her most devoted fans are younger audiences whose problems she deals with in her works (particularly the confusing experiences of young girls growing up). In 2006 she made her playwriting debut with *Var är alla [Where is Everyone?]*, a play about what happens when erotic charge gets out of hand.

About the Translator

Kari Dickson was born in Edinburgh, Scotland, and grew up bilingually, as her mother is Norwegian and her grandparents could not speak English. She has a B.A. in Scandinavian studies and an M.A. in translation. She worked in theatre in London and Oslo before becoming a translator. She is also a part-time tutor in Scandinavian studies at the University of Edinburgh.

Stone Tree

Gyrðir Elíasson

Translated from the Icelandic by Victoria Cribb

ISBN 9781905583089
RRP: £7.99

** *Winner of the 2011 Nordic Council Literature Prize* **

Gyrðir Elíasson's stories take us out of ourselves. Situated on the lonely western shores of Iceland, or out in the vast mountain ranges or barren lava fields of this spectacular country, each one is a study in self-exile. We follow a Boston ornithologist, speeding through the landscape in a fourby-four, chasing Arctic Terns; a schoolboy relocating to the northernmost town of Siglufjördur to compete in a chess tournament; a husband packing his wife off to visit her aunt in Sweden. In almost every story we find people taking leave of their normal lives in order to take their dreams more seriously.

Praise for *Stone Tree*:

'In vivid and haunting prose, Eliasson shows how no man can be an island, as community intrudes upon their self-exile in the most unexpected ways.'
- *The Independent on Sunday*

www.commapress.co.uk

The Madman of Freedom Square

Hassan Blasim

Translated from the Arabic by Jonathan Wright

978-1905583256£7.99

'Perhaps the best writer of Arabic fiction alive...'
— The Guardian

From hostage-video makers in Baghdad, to human trafficking in the forests of Serbia, institutionalised paranoia in the Saddam years, to the nightmares of an exile trying to embrace a new life in Amsterdam... Blasim's stories present an uncompromising view of the West's relationship with Iraq, spanning over twenty years and taking in everything from the Iran-Iraq War through to the Occupation, as well as offering a haunting critique of the post-war refugee experience.

'Blasim moves adeptly between surreal, internalised states of mind and ironic commentary on Islamic extremism and the American invasion... excellent.'
— *The Metro*

'Blasim pitches everyday horror into something almost gothic... his taste for the surreal can be Gogol-like.'
— *The Independent*

'At first you receive it with the kind of shocked applause you'd award a fairly transgressive stand-up. You're quite elated.'
— M John Harrison.

Long Days

Maike Wetzel

Translated from the German by Lyn Marven

978-1905583027
£7.95

'Recently something funny happened. There was no summer, no autumn either.'

With this opener Maike Wetzel begins exploring that moment in life when the breakneck experience of growing up suddenly changes gear and slows down. A young woman sees a dead body for the first time; a sister watches her anorexic sibling transform into different person; a girl pieces together the facts of a custody battle she's not been let in on. Wetzel's stories catch people when some part of their lives has been put on pause, leaving them so adrift only acts of obsession or self-destruction provide direction.

'A fantastic collection of short stories from one of Europe's most promising young writers'
— *Bellistra*

'There is the special art in Maike Wetzel's writing to demonstrate vividly how events and stories can affect people — in particular if those only passively involved.'
— *Der Spiegel*

'Adds magic to the brutal banality of everyday-life.'
— *Schlaglicht*

www.commapress.co.uk

I Love You When I'm Drunk

Empar Moliner

Translated from the Catalan by Peter Bush

978 1905583058
£7.95

Fast, precise, hilariously timed and mercilessly honest, the stories of Empar Moliner lay bare every pretension ever to have offered comfort to the middle class psyche. From the zeal of a mothers' group staging a world record breastfeeding attempt to couples role-playing their way into parenthood at a third world 'adoption workshop', every well-meaning fad and right-on gesture is brilliantly observed and astutely exposed.

'Deft and ingenious'
— *Times Literary Supplement*

'With a fresh and direct language and great humour, Moliner takes the logic of small, everyday situations to their limit'
— *Lift Stuttgart*

www.commapress.co.uk